OPERATION
GRIZZLY
CAMP

a Poppy McVie adventure

Titles by Kimberli A. Bindschatel

The Poppy McVie Series
Operation Tropical Affair
Operation Orca Rescue
Operation Grizzly Camp

The Fallen Shadows Trilogy
The Path to the Sun (Book One)

OPERATION
GRIZZLY
CAMP

KIMBERLI A. BINDSCHATEL

Turning Leaf · Traverse City, MI

Published by Turning Leaf Productions, LLC.
Traverse City, Michigan

www.PoppyMcVie.com
www.KimberliBindschatel.com

Print ISBN-13:9780996189057
Print ISBN-10:099618905X

Thank you for purchasing this book and supporting an indie author.

For Kathleen—
Thank you for teaching me how to be a friend.

And to the brave men and women of the U.S.F.W.S. and their counterparts around the globe who dedicate their lives to save animals from harm. Their courage and commitment is nothing short of inspiring.

May their efforts not be in vain.

Change happens by listening and then starting a dialogue with the people who are doing something you don't believe is right.

~Dr. Jane Goodall

OPERATION
GRIZZLY
CAMP

KIMBERLI A. BINDSCHATEL

CHAPTER 1

Across the airport terminal, through the blur of hurried travelers between us, I caught sight of Dalton, facing the other way. There was no mistaking him, the way he fit in a pair of jeans. *Ooooh my*. He turned and saw me, waved me over with a smile, but as I approached I could tell by the way his eyes held mine that something was up.

Special Agent Dalton had been my partner now for nearly six months, but not without some fireworks between us. I'd learned that when he was in this mood, the best strategy was to take a deep breath and find my inner calm. I'd yet to be successful, but hey, a girl can try.

Our relationship had come a long way in a short time. I trusted him with my life. As an agent, he was top-notch. He was sharp, experienced, everything you'd want in a partner. The trouble was, he set me on fire—in more ways than one. I was still trying to figure out how I felt about him. I was pretty sure he had feelings for me. The problem was, with Dalton, well, it was complicated.

Despite our…I don't even know what to call it, we'd just had two successful ops and now, without so much as a two-day breather, we were heading to Alaska on a mission to catch a bear poacher who'd been eluding authorities for years. That's how things work out sometimes. Get 'em when the gettin's good.

I set down my duffel bag between us. "What is it?"

"Hey Poppy." He paused for a beat. "Alaska, here we come," he said with a forced grin.

"Seriously?" I planted my feet. "I know that look."

He hooked his thumb in his belt, looked down at his shoes.

"Oh my god, Dalton. Spit it out."

His eyes made their way back to meet mine. "Stan Martin called me yesterday."

"Stan Martin? As in the head of Special Ops, Stan Martin? Our boss?" *Crap. This can't be good.* "And?"

"He wants me to come in for an official interview—" his tongue stuck in the corner of his mouth for a moment "—an investigative hearing actually, on—" he stared at me "—on what happened during our op in Norway."

My brain started to swirl around inside my skull. "I don't understand. It was a clean bust."

"I know. I know." Dalton nodded, too much. "I'm sure it's all a formality. Politics, you know. Apparently Norway officials have been making a stink about it."

"Well, when does he want us to come in?"

Dalton managed a half-shrug.

My brain rattled. *Investigative hearing.* The roar of the airline passengers hustling past rose in my ears and suddenly made me feel dizzy. I sucked in some air. *Oh crap.* "It's about me."

Dalton held up a hand, a caution to stay calm. "I don't know that for sure."

"Of course you do." I blew out my breath. "What'd he say exactly?"

He looked away.

"C'mon."

"He might have mentioned that he's not sure you understand procedures, protocol, that kind of thing."

I held myself erect, forced calm. "I know I pushed the

envelope a little. Maybe taken it right to the edge." *Dammit.* "Okay, maybe a little over. But who doesn't? It was all legal. In the end. We nailed Ray Goldman, his most-wanted. We caught the bad guy and I'm proud of it."

"I know." He nodded some more. "It's just that, I think the thing is, you're still, technically, in probationary training and it's standard procedure to—"

I shook my head. "There's nothing standard about it. You said it's an investigative hearing. So stop sugar-coating it."

Dalton sighed, his shoulders slumped. "He used the words brazen, greenhorn, half-cocked, and—" he hesitated "—lone wolf."

I looked down at my hands and drew in a long breath to keep myself from exploding. My left hand turned white where my right one wrung the life out of it. "I don't understand. I nailed the guy and—" My jaw tensed when I realized what I'd said. "*We* nailed him." *Crap. This can't be happening.* "You were on board the whole time. You approved everything. We were in it together and—"

"Yes, I did." He gave me an encouraging smile. "Don't worry. I'm you're partner. I've got your back."

I let myself relax a little. In spite of all the things I was still unsure of with Dalton, I trusted him. He wouldn't lie to me.

"Well, what's going to happen? Will I be suspended?" I couldn't lose my job. It was everything. Everything I'd ever wanted. I'd worked hard to get where I was. And now it was at risk. Everything on the line. Because I was unorthodox, different, creative. Because I'd done it my way. Same old story.

Now I'd be summoned to the office of Stan Martin, head of Special Ops. My heart raced like a little rabbit being led into the cave of the fierce and almighty king-of-the-jungle.

"I don't know. But I told Martin I couldn't come in until after this op in Alaska is done. It's too important. That will give us some time to go over the details, make sure our report was solid, our stories match."

"All right." Now I was the one nodding like a bobble-head.

I picked up the duffle bag, ready to get out of here. I had things to think about, to sort out.

I looked to Dalton and pasted a smile on my face.

He eyed me, still tense. There was something else. I dropped the duffle. "There's more?"

His tongue went back to the same corner of his mouth. Then I realized: he only had one gun case. He was supposed to pick up firearms for both of us.

"Where's my gun?" I took a step back. "Don't tell me—" *No. No, no, no!* "I'm already suspended?"

"Huh?" He glanced down at the gun case he'd set on the floor. "No, I put them in one case. For weight. On the small plane later."

"Oh." I let out my breath. "Then what is it? You're killing me here."

He stared at me for a long moment, then seemed to come to a decision. "Are you ready for this op?"

"Ready? Of course I'm ready. I mean, I'm a little worried now, about the Martin thing but—why are you asking me that?"

"I just need to know, you know, if you're ready. I want to make sure, I mean, with everything going on, that you're up for it. That it's what you really want to do. You know, this kind of op, with all the ins and outs of it. I mean, it's a different kind of situation and—"

"Now you're babbling." *What the hell?*

"What?" He drew back, defensive. "I don't babble."

"You do. And you are. What's your point?"

He frowned, hands on his hips. Then he ran his fingers through his hair, the way he does when he's thinking, leaving it a little ruffled.

I melted a little. That hair. *Not the time. Focus.*

"It's a hunting trip. We're going hunting."

"I know that."

"But you've got to be able to play the part." His expression turned stern. "I know you're against hunting."

"I am not." *Well, not exactly.* "I think hunting is...well, most hunters. I mean..."

"Yeah?" Those eyes stared at me, waiting. Those ever-so-tempting, knock-me-flat eyes. The way he'd look at me sometimes—just a glance made my insides flutter. Downright embarrassing. *Focus!*

"I understand hunting for food. I get it. I don't like it, but I don't condemn it either. I—" *be honest* "—accept it. Honestly, if you're going to eat meat, hunting is more humane than factory farming and—"

"I know. I've heard you say it. Many times. But I'm not convinced. And it doesn't matter anyway, this op isn't about sustenance hunting. We're talking about *bear* hunting."

I pursed my lips together.

"Well?"

"Oh all right. It's abhorrent. To hunt a predator, just for the sake of killing, to brag about the conquest, make the hide into a fur rug to show off your prowess, or whatever reason people do it, it's barbaric. It's just plain murder."

"You see." He rocked back on his heels, crossed his arms. "That's exactly my point."

"But that's why we're going."

"That's *not* why we're going." He stepped closer, lowered his voice. "We're not going to bust bear hunters, Poppy. We're not activists with Greenpeace. We're federal agents and bear hunting is legal, whether you like it or not." He paused. "Our directive is to catch them poaching. There's a difference."

"I know there's a difference." *Under the law.* "And yes,

I have my issues with hunting. What's your point? Are you questioning my ability to do my job?"

He stared, blinked, then blinked again as if he were carefully choosing his next words. "I'm just thinking that maybe this is too personal."

I drew back, anger bubbling up. "Because of my dad?"

"I know this must—"

"Yes, he was killed by poachers. Yes, I'm angry about it. But that doesn't mean I can't do my job." I crossed my arms. "If you think I'm not qualified, fine. Or Joe thinks our cover is weak, fine. But my dad's file is confidential. You had no right to read it."

His eyes turned soft from...what? Guilt? Compassion?

He looked away, then back. "I was told to."

"By whom?"

He gave me the you-know-who frown.

I turned away. Of course my boss would know about it. I'm a federal agent. They'd done a full background check when I applied. But that didn't mean he had a right to show it to Dalton.

The file didn't give the full story. At best, it was a few, scant reports from the investigators, low-level government employees who'd arrived on the scene days after his murder. It was Africa. The politics of an American killed by poachers could get out of control, so justice didn't matter as much as keeping the peace.

My dad's murder was declared inconclusive, lacking evidence, likely an accident, though anyone who knew anything about the situation knew exactly who had killed him and why. The whole thing made my dad look like an idiot. It was a load of crap.

"That report was bullshit. My dad was murdered."

"No doubt," he said and meant it.

My resolve softened. I looked him in the eye. "I don't hate

poachers because a few killed my dad. I hate poachers because they poach."

He nodded in understanding.

"It's not going to affect my job. I swear it."

He held my gaze. "You say that but—" He shook his head.

"But what?" God, he was exasperating!

He leaned toward me. "What's rule number one when undercover?"

Eye roll. "Never break your cover."

"Right." His eyes narrowed. His tone turned dead serious. "Your cover is a trophy hunter and an unethical one at that. Not only do you need to cozy up to these men, you need to act like you actually like them. No doubt you can. But that's just the half of it. Much more important is when you're in the field, gun in your hand, with a bear in your sights, will you pull the trigger?" His eyes bored into me. "Because that's what we're doing. That's where we're going. That's the job. Are you ready for that?"

My teeth clenched together. "You don't need to tell me my job."

His eyes flared with frustration.

I stared right back at him. "You assume—" I paused, thinking for a beat. I needed to find the right words.

"I know that mind of yours. You're thinking of ways around it. You think you can outsmart them. And maybe you can. But right now, you're under the microscope. The head of Special Ops is watching. You. Me. And I'm only willing to go so far. I'm not going to lie to him. This is it, Poppy."

I set my jaw, reached down and picked up my duffel bag. "Well, you don't have to worry, *partner*. I'll do my job."

Chapter 2

I turned my back on Dalton as I slid into my large, cushy, first-class seat then gave him a little wave as he passed toward the back of the plane. "See you in Anchorage."

Having a best friend who's a flight attendant for the airlines comes in handy. He'd upgraded me. Actually, Chris was more like family. With my life changing so dramatically lately, being called to Special Ops, off to Costa Rica, then right away to Norway, I admit, I'd neglected him. I owed him a phone call, some time together. Yep, as soon as I got back from this op, I was going to schedule a couple days to see him. A big thank you dinner was in order. Maybe a bottle of his favorite Malbec.

I exhaled. *Dalton*. What was I going to do about Dalton?

And this thing at headquarters. Investigative hearing. What did that even mean anyway?

I leaned my head back and took a deep breath. Right now I needed to set all that aside and focus on the mission at hand: Operation Grizzly Camp.

We were heading to Alaska to rendevous with Joe Nash, our supervisor and Special Agent in Charge, on an op to catch a bear poacher he'd been courting for years, practically his entire career. The elusive Mark Townsend. The State boys had given up. This guy knew all of them by name and knew every loophole. He'd become untouchable. Part of the reason was he never took new clients. Well, almost never. Joe had found a way in: me. The guy liked the lady hunters, especially daughters. It ensured, in his mind, that the men weren't law enforcement. Having me on board was Joe's ticket. Of course I was thrilled to play along.

My cover was the daughter of a wealthy trophy-hunter (Joe, of course) from Oklahoma, land of tornadoes, rodeos, and bubblin' crude. Oil that is, black gold, the stuff that lines our pockets and funds our adventures. And adventures we shall have. We're out to collect every big game trophy on every continent. Daddy's building a wing on the house to display every one of them, so any time I want, I can relive the moment, the moment when that animal breathed its last breath, when I conquered it and could call it mine.

Egads. How do these people stand themselves? That was enough prepping. I didn't want to drive my head into a black hole of depression. I'd wing it when I got there.

I glanced around the first-class cabin, quickly assessing the other passengers. Some of the other hunters staying at the lodge we were headed to might be on this plane.

Directly behind me sat a man and woman with graying hair, wearing those oversized, square-lensed sunglasses on their heads, the kind that fit over regular glasses. The woman fondled a homemade, quilted handbag stuffed to the gills that rested in her lap. Definitely not hunters. Tourists, most likely, going to catch the train south to Seward to board one of the many monster-sized cruise ships that sailed the Inside Passage.

A flight attendant, whom I assumed was the purser since she'd already served a few drinks to other first-class passengers, came down the aisle, checking on passengers. She was a slim woman, her uniform perfectly pressed. Yep, she was in charge. "Your bag needs to fit down at your feet or go in an overhead compartment," she chirped as she passed by.

The woman shifted and moaned, trying to shove it below the seat.

"I told you not to bring all that crap," the man grumbled.

"Oh George, don't start with me."

"There's room in the overhead," I said, getting to my feet. "I'd be happy to put it up there for you."

"Oh, aren't you sweet," she said, trying to lift it over George to hand it to me.

George crossed his arms with a harumph as I took the bag and lifted it into the storage compartment. I gave him a big smile. See if a little sugar could melt that heart.

I made a quick scan of the other passengers before I sat back down in my seat. On the other side of the aisle, two men, also in the row behind me, looked like possibilities — morning stubble, camo baseball caps, flannel shirts. Once we were in the air, I would be able to hear them talking. I could even strike up a conversation with them. They couldn't have been five years older than me. A little flirting might do the trick.

The woman seated next to me, by the window, sat upright with the posture of a 1950s debutante and had the hairdo to match, all pinned and coiffed.

With my Oklahoma accent, which I'd been practicing for a couple weeks, I asked, "What takes you to Alaska today?"

A warm smile spread across her face. "Visiting my grandchildren. My son is in the service, stationed in Anchorage. And where are you going, my dear?"

"Oh, I'm heading out to the backcountry."

"Well, you be careful. There are bears everywhere, you know." She patted the back of my hand. "Make sure you wear bells on your shoes."

I stifled a grin. Someone, somewhere had come up with the notion that wearing little bells would scare bears away. No doubt some ambitious souvenir vendor. Sure, you wanted to make your presence known, avoid startling a wild animal, but little jingly bells tied to your shoelaces were more likely to arouse curiosity than to actually scare away a bear. Bells aren't terribly loud and the jingling is easily lost on the wind or amid the sounds of the forest. It's much more effective to use your own voice.

"I won't need any bells," I said with a grin. Then, loud enough for the men behind me to hear, "I'll have my Ruger 375 H&H Mag rifle. I'm taking me home a trophy."

Her face turned stone-like and her lips made a tiny pucker.

Yeah, I'm with you, Grandma.

She slowly reached into the seat pocket, pulled out the in-flight magazine, and with a curt smile, turned her attention to it.

Well played, Grandma. Well played.

I turned in my seat, caught the eye of one of the hunters, and gave him a little you-get-it shrug.

He nodded and asked, "Where are you headed?"

The man seated next to him leaned in to hear my reply.

Gotcha. "A lodge near Katmai. Hunting bear." They both nodded, as if they knew where that was. "You?"

"North of Fairbanks," the one said. "We've got two more flights after this one."

I could see now, by their eyes, they were brothers. The one chattered on. "Bears are fun, but a bull moose in rut, whew-weee, now there's a beast to reckon with."

The other one chimed in. "What my brother means is, statistically, you're more likely to get attacked by a moose than a bear. Here in Alaska about ten people are wounded or killed by moose annually."

The woman behind me leaned over her husband to join the conversation. "Are you sayin' them moose is dangerous? I thought them were big deer. They's just grazers, ain't they?"

"They are," the first brother replied. "Deer that weigh fifteen-hundred pounds with spiked antlers that span six feet." He held his hands up in the air, spreading them wide. "A moose gets fired up in the rut, he'll plow down half the forest to get to you. If one comes after you, run like hell."

"A moose can outrun you though," the other brother added, his face full of life. They were all fired up.

"Yeah, you'll want to zigzag between big trees."

"Zigzag?" she said, incredulous.

He nodded. "Zig zag. They don't corner well. Kinda top heavy."

"So you're on a moose hunting trip, I take it?" I asked.

Their heads bobbed, grins taking over their faces. They were downright giddy.

The first brother's eyes lit up. "We've been planning this trip our whole lives. We can't wait to take one down."

I hid my dismay behind a cordial smile. These men's lifelong dream was to kill a living being. A beautiful, magnificent creature. To chop it down. Rather than be thoughtful, introspective, they were bouncing in their seats. I really wanted to slap some compassion into them. Instead, I did my job and stayed in character. "Boy, that sounds exciting. You been hunting your whole lives?"

"Yep," the first brother answered. "We own a family ranch in Texas." The other brother dug around in his pockets for his wallet while the first kept talking. "A game farm. Two hundred fifty acres."

The brother handed me a business card that read: Wilson's Hunting Ranch. Giraffes, Kangaroos, Deer & More! Native & Exotic. 40+ Species for Hunt. 100% Success Rate. Book a hunt today!

My mind stuck on the size of the ranch. Two hundred fifty acres. Hunting there, if you could call it that, would be like shooting fish in a barrel. These brothers sold canned hunts. Whatever animal the *hunter* wanted they'd release from a cage into a small fenced area, so it could be shot on the spot.

I looked up at them, lost for words. Their whole lives

revolved around killing. I could hardly stomach any more. "Well, good luck," I said and started to turn around in my seat when I saw Chris, zipping down the aisle toward me from the back of the plane. I didn't know he'd actually be on the flight. A smile spread across my face.

He gave me a wink. *Crap.* My eyes went right to the hunters. I had to be careful. "I need your seat belts buckled," Chris said as he blew through. I couldn't believe it. He'd rearranged his schedule to be on my flight.

The man behind me gave his wife a look of disgust. "Of all the stewardesses in the world, we get this candyass," he said aloud while he took his sweet time fastening his seatbelt.

His wife's cheeks turned pink and her eyes dropped to her hands.

Asshole. I swung around and faced forward. Chris dealt with bigotry all the time, and always with class, it was one of the things I admired about him, but it got my cockles up. I tried to push it out of my mind. And the hunters and their lust for killing. What was it with this world?

I pulled out the in-flight magazine and stared at the pages, not reading a word. *Focus on the op.* Mark Townsend was his name. And we were going to nail him.

So sit back and enjoy the flight.

The aircraft pushed back from the gate. We were headed north.

No matter how many times I fly, I still love that sensation when the plane goes racing down the runway, the landing gear rattling and shaking, as the sheer power of the jet engines thrusts me back into my seat. Then there's that moment, that tiny, precious moment, when the wheels leave the ground and I'm airborne. Defying gravity. Freedom.

As we climbed and climbed, I leaned over to see out the window. All I saw, for miles and miles, was a landscape sectioned off in green and brown squares, with lines and lines of concrete roads, crisscrossing in intricate patterns. Amazing how we've carved and shaped and formed the earth to fit our needs. No part of this world has gone untouched, unaltered. I fear we'll regret it someday when all the animals are gone, and the ecosystems are damaged beyond repair, ecosystems we rely on more than we can possibly comprehend.

Over billions of years, the earth has come to a beautiful ecological balance, one where humans have thrived. Mess with it too much and we won't. Simple as that. Why doesn't everyone see what we're doing to this world?

Once the captain turned off the seatbelt sign, Chris came to my seat. "The purser would like to speak with you. Would you follow me?"

"Sure," I said with a shrug.

He led me to the galley area up front, just behind the cockpit and hidden from the view of most of the passengers.

"This is a full flight," he whispered. "I had to do some serious negotiating to get you in first-class."

I wrapped my arms around him in a big hug. I didn't realize until now how much I'd missed him. "Thanks, you know I appreciate it, but why didn't you tell me you were going to be on the flight?"

"I wanted to surprise you. I've never been to Anchorage and we haven't seen each other in forever and you've been so distracted and—"

"Oh Chris." I hugged him again then lowered my voice, "Just remember, I'm undercover and I—"

"I know. I know. I just—we haven't talked in a long time." He paused, drew in a breath. "You know, talked."

"What? We talk all the time on the phone."

"Yeah, but, well, you talk, but I just really, you know." He sighed. "It's just that I have something I've been wanting to tell you. In person."

"What? What's happened? Are you okay?"

He chewed on his bottom lip. "I guess I didn't think this through."

"Now you have me worried. What is it?"

He frowned. "Everything is great. I promise. It's good news." He stared at me for a moment with an intensity I hadn't seen for a long time, then shook his head. "I shouldn't have come. You're undercover right now. It can wait until after you get back."

"Are you sure? Because I can—"

"No, really. How long will you be gone?"

"Two weeks."

"Perfect." He smiled, satisfied. "We'll plan to get together then. You'll take a few days off, right? Promise me."

"Absolutely."

"Not some quick layover lunch. Mexico. For a real, honest-to-goodness va-cay. You need to take a deep breath and I need a long-deserved break. Beach, cocktails, sunshine. You got me?"

I nodded. "I can't wait." I gave him a kiss on the cheek, then started back toward my seat, but turned around. I had to know. "One little hint?"

"It's all right. Honestly. It can wait." A grin creeped across his face. "But I almost forgot. I got you something." He pulled a bag from a galley cabinet and handed it to me.

Inside was a jacket. Pink camouflage. "You didn't!" I grinned.

"I did." He snickered. "I couldn't resist."

"This is god-awful tacky."

He tried to contain a full-out giggle. "It's perfect."

A smirk came to my lips. "You're bad."

"I know."

I put it on. Snuggly fleece.

"I got you something else," he said. From his pocket, he handed me a tiny box.

"What is this?"

"Open it," he said. "And hurry up. I've actually got to work on this flight."

"I mean, what's it for? It's not my birthday or anything."

"I just"—he shrugged—"wanted you to have it."

Inside the box was a silver chain with a pendant—a tiny compass.

"To help you find your way," he said, his eyes all moist, which got my eyes all moist. *Oh Chris*. "I mean, I know it doesn't actually work—"

"I love it."

"It's just that you've been, well…"

Suddenly my throat stuck shut. "Oh god, Chris, what am I going to do if I get fired?"

"What?" He jerked backward. "What are you talking about?" His eyes softened. "Oh my god, you're serious. What's happened?"

I shook my head. "I can't talk about it right now."

"Whoa, whoa, whoa. Wait a minute. Dalton's probably just gotten a little hot under the collar. I'm sure if you talk to him—"

"Not Dalton." I puckered. "Stan Martin. Head of Special Ops."

"Head of—what the hell? Poppy! What did you do?"

"Nothing!"

He gave me that look.

"Dalton got called for an investigative hearing on our op in Norway. They're investigating me."

His hand went to cover his mouth. "Oh shit, girl. That ain't good."

"Dalton says not to worry, it's all politics, but—" I clamped my lips together. "If I make one mistake, one bad move, one slip on this op with Joe, it's all over."

"Okay, now I'm confused. I thought you said the *head* of

Special Ops. Joe's your boss. But isn't he Joe's boss?"

"Well, yeah, but that's not the point. I mean, it's Joe's op, so—I just need to—"

"You need to take a deep breath." He pulled me to him, wrapped his arms around me. "It'll be okay. Trust Dalton. I'm sure he's right. If this Martin guy is the head of the department, he's getting his ass chewed about something and he's got to pass it down the line. It'll probably blow over."

"I don't know. He's summoned Dalton for an interview and I don't know if he'll—"

Chris pulled away to look me in the eye. "Dalton's a lot of things, but he's no snitch. He'll stand up for you."

I nodded. "I know. You're right. You're always right. But it's just that…"

"Just what?"

"He knows about my dad. He's questioning whether I can do my job because of it."

Chris took hold of me by the shoulders. "You're the strongest woman I know. And the smartest. What happened to your dad has no bearing on that."

I managed a smile.

He took the necklace from the box, held it around my neck, and hooked the clasp.

I fingered the tiny compass, trying to find words. I looked into his eyes and was sure that he knew that I would lose it if I stood there any longer. "I should get back to my seat."

He nodded. "I need to get to the back and set up the cart service."

He shoved the empty shopping bag into the cabinet. As he turned, I thrust my arms around him again. "I love you."

"Me too," he said as he nudged my chin with his, just like my dad used to do. It made me smile and relax a little. "Everything's going to be okay. So don't go getting all sappy on me now. You're a big, bad hunter. Let's go."

I grinned and headed back to my seat, Chris right behind me. The old lady saw me coming and looked away. As I turned to slide into the seat, I noticed the man behind my seat's eyes fixed on Chris. I lingered, standing in front of my seat, as Chris passed me.

The man put out his arm to block his way. "I want another Jack and Coke."

Chris smiled his hospitality smile and said, "I'll let the purser know, sir," then tried to continue down the aisle, but the man grabbed him by the arm.

"You can get it for me. You're a stewardess, ain't ya?"

My pulse rate shot into the stratosphere.

Chris calmly responded over his shoulder. "The purser takes care of first-class. She'd be happy to get your drink. I'll let her know right away."

The man yanked Chris's arm, pulling him backward. "You'll do it now, fag."

I brain caught on fire. "Hey, hands off, mister!"

The man scowled and started to rise from the seat but got caught by the seatbelt. His face flushed red. He flicked the buckle open. "How dare you, girl," he growled, rising from his seat with surprising strength. He still had a grip on Chris's arm, tugging him.

I pushed into the aisle, chopped at the asshole's wrist with my forearm, breaking his grip on Chris. I latched on and twisted his arm back into an arm bar. "I said hands off." His face turned beet red.

Chris had his hands in the air. "It's all right. No harm done. Let him go."

I twisted harder. The man clenched his teeth and glared at me.

"Now say you're sorry," I hissed.

He lifted his free hand as though to slap me across the face, but the two hunters were on their feet behind me.

"The lady's right," the one brother said. "You were out of line there, Mister."

The man hesitated before easing back into his seat, his eyes on the brothers.

The brother nodded toward my hands where I still had the man's arm pinned back. "I think you've made your point."

I released my grip.

The purser appeared behind me, all perky smiles. "Everything all right here?"

The other brother piped up. "This man was choking on a pretzel, but he's fine now."

With a suspicious nod, the purser slowly turned before heading back to the front of the plane.

"Thank you," I whispered to the brother, filled with shame for how I'd judged him before.

Dalton came up behind Chris. "What the hell's going on, Sis?"

Shit.

"I'll get your drink right away, sir," Chris said. He turned to me, glaring. "Would you kindly get back in your seat?"

I glanced around the cabin. Everyone was silent, staring.

Dalton pushed past Chris and hustled me toward the front of the plane to the galley. "What the hell is wrong with you?"

"I...I just—"

He shook his head. "You just what? Dammit, Poppy."

I held up my hands. "I know. I know."

"What the hell were you thinking?"

"Nothing. I wasn't. I just, he was harassing Chris." I leaned closer and said through clenched teeth, "He called him a fag."

He spun around, hands on his hips. "Is that all? Do you not understand what it means to be undercover?"

"Yes, and I don't need a lecture."

"Apparently you do."

Chris poked his head around the corner. "What the hell, Poppy? Are you trying to get me fired?"

"What? No. Why would—"

"I got you in first-class. Under my company ID! You know the rules, the code of conduct."

Shit.

Chris flung open a drawer, mixed the Jack and Coke, then stomped off.

Dalton looked me up and down, shaking his head. "You'd better get your shit together."

Four and a half hours later, my nose dry and tongue like sandpaper, the plane banked right and started to descend. Chris hadn't said another word to me the entire flight. I owed him an apology, big time. Dalton was right. I did need to get my shit together, like he said, as clichéd as that might be. It was one thing to have my own job on the line for my impulsive behavior, but I'd put Chris's at risk too—oh, what was I thinking?

And Dalton. He'd just warned me about this very thing. I'd probably ruined any chance of us being able to work together again. That is, if I still had a job after this op. Maybe it wouldn't matter anyway.

I was tempted to start belting down some Jack and Cokes myself.

The plane banked again and we leveled off for the approach to the Ted Stevens Anchorage International Airport, the third-busiest cargo traffic airport in the world. Snow-capped mountains spread out forever in several directions. Cook Inlet provided a dazzling reflection of the Anchorage skyline, a metropolis the size of Delaware with a population exceeding 400,000, right smack in the middle of pristine, unending wilderness.

One of the many advantages of flying first-class is not having to wait for everyone else to deplane. Once on the ground and the door opened, I grabbed my duffle and bolted.

At the end of the jetbridge, I spotted a Cinnabon and figured standing in line there was the perfect place to watch for the man and his wife, see if he made a complaint to the airline agent greeting passengers as they filed past. Besides, I was in the mood for some sugar therapy.

I watched the couple as they stopped to catch their breath after huffing up the jetway then passed by the agent and headed toward the bathroom. Maybe I'd get lucky and that was the end of it.

Dalton sauntered up to me looking like he'd just woke from a refreshing nap. *SEALs.*

"Well, look at you. As fresh as a daisy," I said.

"Am I?" he said, looking down at his shirt. "And I wasn't the one in first class."

"Yeah, well." I frowned.

His eyes fixed on the Cinnabon case. "Seriously?"

"I thought it was a good place to keep a lookout." I made a subtle nod toward the jetway. "See if he files a complaint."

"Yeah? And what will you do if he does?"

I shrugged. I had no answer.

"You don't have to make an excuse if you want a cinnamon bun."

"Look what I'm wearing." I tugged at the pink camouflage.

He grinned. "It suits you."

"Funny." I smirked. "Anyone who'd seriously wear this would beeline for a Cinnabon."

"Uh huh."

"Really. It fits my cover."

"Yep." His lip curved up at the edge. His half-grin, I called it. Irresistible.

"You're so aggravating."

"If you say so."

I gritted my teeth. He was. Aggravating, that is. At least he was talking to me now.

Once I had downed half that bun of oozy, gooey sweetness, my stomach did a barrel roll in objection. I puffed out my cheeks, feeling stuffed.

Dalton shook his head. "Shall we get our baggage now?"

"You still here?"

I spun around. It was Chris. His eyes dropped to the remains of the Cinnabun in my hand.

"I'm sorry, Chris. I don't know what I was thinking." I held out the bun to him. An offering.

"Do you think a Cinnabun is going to fix it?" He glared at me, hands on his hips.

"No." I hung my head. "Do you think he'll—"

"I doubt it," he said as he snatched the bun from my hand and tore off a bite. "I kept serving him Double Jack and Cokes. I don't think he's in the mood to make a complaint. Besides, I don't think his wife was very happy with him either."

I nodded and stood there in the uncomfortable silence.

Chris held out his hand to Dalton. "I'm Chris, by the way. We haven't been formally introduced."

"Oh, I'm sorry," I said with a quick look around to make sure no one was within earshot. "This is my partner, Special Agent—" I paused for emphasis "—G. Dalton. Yep, you heard me. I don't actually know his first name."

Dalton gave me the tiniest smirk. "Just Dalton," he said to Chris.

Somehow, without my noticing during the introductions, the three of us had started walking. Chris chattered on about air travel or something. My head was lost in a sugar haze.

Near baggage claim, Chris stopped in front of a giant glass-encased grizzly bear. The animals stood on its hind legs, its mouth forced into a permanent roar. "Holy shit! Are they really that big? That thing's ferocious."

"It's a world record take," Dalton said. "Bigger than most."

"Yeah, but still." Chris shuddered. "You're going to be out there in the wilderness with those? What if one decides you'd be a tasty lunch?"

Dalton eyed Chris, shaking his head. "Don't worry, I'll be with her the whole time."

What was it with these two? "I can take care of myself."

Dalton went on as if I hadn't said anything. "The thing about bears is, if they do charge, it's often a bluff. Eight times out of ten. The key is to never run."

"A bear comes after me, my skinny ass is outta there."

"Not if you want to survive," Dalton told him. "If you run, you'll incite the bear to chase. They can sprint thirty-five miles per hour." He grinned. "I don't think you can hit forty."

I added. "Dalton's right. But generally you don't have to worry. They're the ultimate predator, yes, but their diet mostly consists of roots and grasses, berries and nuts, and salmon in the fall."

"Define *mostly*," Chris said, deadpan.

"I'm just saying. They're not the ferocious killers people make them out to be. They're really fascinating, actually. Did you know that a bear's sense of smell is seven times more powerful than a bloodhound's?"

Dalton tapped on the glass case, pointing to a plaque inside. "Look here." It read: World record Kodiak Brown bear (*ursus arctos middendorffi*) Skull score - 30 10/16 inches, harvested on April 20, 1997.

"Harvested?" Chris said, eyebrows raised.

I rolled my eyes. "Like a field of wheat." I leaned toward Chris. "The poor bear was probably snoozing when he shot it. Then it gets mounted in that heinous pose."

Dalton gave me a look.

I frowned. *I know.*

I stared up at the bear, into his glass eyes, and imagined meeting his real gaze in the wild. This beautiful creature once lived, breathed, walked the woods in all his majesty. Digging for clams with those six inch claws. And those teeth. Ripping a spawning salmon apart for the roe.

"I don't understand it," Chris said.

"Don't understand what?" Dalton asked.

"Bear hunting. I mean, I get wanting to feed your family, all that. But to go after a bear like that? Look at the size of that monster. His teeth. Those claws."

"It's a testosterone thing," Dalton said.

Chris turned to me, eyebrows raised in his playful way. "Is that supposed to be an insult?"

"No, nope, uh uh," Dalton stuttered. "Not at all."

"He means it makes them feel manly," I said. "Killing something. Something powerful."

"Yeah? Then why would a twenty-four year old girl want to hunt one?"

"Yeah, Poppy," Dalton said, glancing around. "You got that one figured out yet?"

I did. Those hours on the plane had given me time to think, to sort some things out. I winked. "It's an adrenaline rush, the thrill of the hunt."

"Now that sounds like you," Chris said and turned to go. "Remember, you owe me. A real vacation in Mexico."

I nodded. Did that mean he'd forgiven me? "I promise. The moment I get back."

His smile turned serious. "Be careful out there. With a beast that powerful," he said, gesturing toward the bear, "you can't be sure who's the hunter and who's the hunted."

CHAPTER 3

Dalton and I got our luggage and walked from the airport terminal, across the road, to the Lake Hood Seaplane Base, where we were to meet our pilot for our floatplane trip to the lodge. Snow-covered mountains and a crisp, blue sky filled with white, puffy clouds made a backdrop for the series of water channels that served as tarmac and runways for this, the busiest seaplane airport in the world. Orange, red, and yellow planes—hundreds of them—lined the side channels, some pulled right up on shore, a few tethered to moorings, all ready to go at a moment's notice. I'd never seen so many small aircraft in one place.

There was no terminal. Just a tiny wood shack next to the dock where the plane was moored. Joe had flown on a different commercial flight and planned to meet up with us there. As we waited, we watched other planes take off every few minutes, their pontoons slapping over the water and throwing spray into the wind.

On my first assignment with Agent Dalton in Costa Rica, Joe had played a rich exotic pet collector, complete with a penchant for expensive cigars and twenty-year-old scotch. Now he was my rich daddy, an oil tycoon intent on taking home a trophy. No doubt, scotch and cigars would play a role this time too.

With his seniority, when he got an op approved, he had a

decent budget to go with it. And boy, did he know how to do it up. When he strolled up to us, he looked the epitome of the part, like he was modeling for the Kuiu huntsmen catalog, with a Tilley waxed-canvas outback hat topping off the ensemble.

"Hi Daddy!" I shouted and gave him a big hug.

"How was your flight, sweetheart?" he asked.

"Long," I said. "I'm so excited to get out there."

I wasn't lying. I was excited.

"Son," he said to Dalton with a fatherly nod.

A man appeared from behind us on the path. "Mr. Pratt, are we ready to head out?"

Joe spun around. "Well, you must be Mr. Townsend. Pleasure to meet you."

The man nodded, shook Joe's hand.

He wasn't at all what I'd expected. Mark Townsend, big-time poacher, the target of our investigation, was a gangly, thin man with a scruffy beard, kind eyes and a wad of chewing tobacco tucked in the side of his bottom lip. "Ma'am," he said to me as he opened the door to the tiny shed. Inside was a large cargo scale. "Put all your bags on there," he said to Dalton.

Once he jotted down the weight, he looked to me with a sheepish expression. "Now I need yours."

"My what?" I asked. I knew what he meant, but I wasn't sure a spoiled college student from Oklahoma would.

"Your weight." He looked to Joe, then Dalton. "All of you."

"Well, I'll be," I said and stepped onto the scale with a frown.

Mark gave me a tolerant grin.

After everyone and all our stuff was weighed and Mark was satisfied, we followed him onto the dock and loaded the plane—a de Havilland Beaver, the workhorse of the Alaskan bush. Bright yellow, her big floats level on top to walk on, she looked like an oversized bathtub toy.

"I want to ride up front, Daddy. Can I ride up front?"

"As long as it's all right with the pilot, sweetheart."

Mark shrugged.

Joe and Dalton squeezed into the tiny backseat and I got into the front passenger seat, opposite Mark, and pulled the door shut, ready to go.

Fascinating how a hunk of metal like this, probably five-thousand pounds, with what I guessed to be a fifty-foot wingspan, could lift off and fly. A commercial jet airliner had enough power to force it into the air. But these little planes were all about aerodynamics, weight versus lift, rudder trim, flaps, all that coming together. I'd always wanted to learn how to fly one.

The dash was a hodgepodge of levers and switches, gauges and buttons, each controlling some small, but no doubt vital part of the equation. On my side, as well as Mark's, there was a yoke and foot pedals. I grabbed the steering apparatus and said, "Hey, I guess I'm the co-pilot, huh?"

Mark's eyes locked on mine. He paused, shifted the lump of chew from one side of his mouth to the other with his tongue before saying, "Don't touch anything."

Here's the thing. What if Mark had a heart attack or choked on his Beech-nut? My life was literally in his hands. At a minimum, I wanted to know how to put this bird back down on the ground. Or at least how to use the radio to call for help. Did that make me a control freak? Or a take-charge kind of person? How about brazen? Half-cocked?

I didn't know what Mr. Martin expected of me. Shouldn't an undercover agent have those qualities? Be a take-charge, grab-the-bull-by-the-horns kind of person?

Trust your team, Dalton would say. Rely on your partner. In this case, trust the expert. But was Townsend the kind of person who'd crumple under stress? What if we hit a flock of birds? What if the engines stalled? Was I supposed to sit back and do nothing? Go down with the plane shouting "See, I'm a good follower!"

Screw that. Mark might not want a co-pilot, but he was getting one.

I glanced around the dash, getting acquainted with what was where. Anything I recognized that is. A GPS locator was mounted in the left corner. The map pocket in my door had an operation manual. That was good.

Mark strapped on his seatbelt. I found mine and clicked it into place. He didn't check to make sure I had my door shut tight, nor did he mention the location of the life vests. Cowboy-type. Good to know.

He flipped a red switch on the dash.

"What's that?" I asked.

He paused, raised one eyebrow, but gave no answer. So that's how it was going to be.

One thing I did know about bush planes: everything is manually operated. With many parts, many things can break or go wrong. In the bush, you want solid components, easy to repair in remote areas with tools that are typically available. No fancy, complicated electronics here.

He handed me a headset, then turned to the guys in the back and motioned for them to put theirs on as well.

Next to his seat, on the left, he pumped a lever or something that made a whoosh, whoosh noise as he pumped, while he simultaneously worked a lever, up and down, on the center console down by his right foot. None of the controls had labels.

"What's that?" I tried again.

He gave me a half grin. "Wobble pump."

"Wobble?" *Very funny.*

More knobs were pushed and levers moved, one labeled throttle, at least that made sense, and the engine turned over and the propeller started spinning.

"Woohoo!" I said. "Let's get going."

Without looking at me, Mark said, "It takes about ten minutes to warm up." He tapped a gauge. "Need forty degrees oil pressure temp, one hundred degrees cylinder head temp."

The plane rattled and shook.

Mark clicked a button on the yoke and started talking on the radio to the control tower. The only part I understood was "requesting departure." He eased the throttle lever forward and as the plane started to move, he pumped a lever on the floor, then some other lever on the dash. He fiddled with some tiny wheels on the ceiling. I was starting to think none of them did anything. Maybe he just had a nervous twitch. Then his eyes met mine. "You ready?" he said with an amused grin.

I nodded.

He reached over and stroked a ragged old rabbit's foot that hung on a tarnished chain from the throttle lever.

Really? Part of a dead animal? *Figures.* "For good luck?" I said.

He grinned. "Out here, you're at the mercy of the wilderness. Sometimes, all you've got is luck."

He pushed the throttle lever all the way forward, the engine roared, and we moved across the water, the floats gliding beneath us. In moments, we were airborne, leaving me wondering how it was possible. We weren't going fast enough to lift a plane into the air. I could have been waterskiing back there. But we were in the air nonetheless.

As soon as we cleared the treetops, Mark turned and winked at me. "You're good luck." He gestured toward the north. "The mountain. She's showing her face today."

I turned. Denali's powerful peaks dominated the horizon, towering over the Alaska Range, dwarfing the surrounding mountains, most of which were as tall as the highest in the Rockies of the lower forty-eight. No wonder its Athabaskan name meant "the Great One."

"Up here, we call it Denali. Crazy bastards come from around the globe to try to climb to the top," Mark said, his voice crackling through the old headset. "It's the fourth highest peak in the world, but I'm told it has the appeal of the highest base-to-summit elevation of any mountain on Earth, rising 18,000 feet from its base. Everest is only a 12,000-foot-climb from its base."

"Really?" I said. "I had no idea."

Mark nodded. "She makes her own weather. The mountain has such mass, she sucks moisture from the Bering Sea and the Gulf of Alaska, stirring up storms year round. Winds average eighty miles per hour on the slope. Add the extreme weather conditions of this arctic climate, which makes for thinner air and a summit temperature commonly at forty degrees below zero." He shook his head. "Not the way I want to meet my maker."

I agreed.

He banked the plane south, along the edge of the Cook Inlet. We were heading for the Alaska peninsula, to a lodge tucked in somewhere near the edge of the Katmai National Park and Preserve.

Below, for miles and miles, vast swaths of nothing but green and white and blue stretched across the landscape. No man-made squares here.

Glacier-covered peaks along the shoreline, dotted with alpine lakes, offered streams that meandered downward, through the patchwork of green, toward the satiny blue sea. Beautiful, untouched, the way it was meant to be. Alaska was truly the last frontier. I held my breath, taking it in.

I glanced at Dalton. He had his head back, sound asleep. I suppose it's the SEAL training. Get sleep when you can. I eased into my seat and closed my eyes. Nope. I sat upright. Too much to see. I leaned on the glass window, so I could see as straight down below us as possible. The sun shimmered off the water, reminding me of a dazzling dinner gown.

After a while, I turned my attention back to Mark. Getting him talking about the hunt might give me some useful information.

"So, we're doing a fly-in hunt, but we'll have a guide, right?" I asked.

"For sure. We'll see how the groups sort out. I've got more than one hunting party at the lodge this week. Full house."

Excellent. We wanted to be put with other hunters, to witness the poaching act. The issue was that most wealthy trophy hunters wanted to hunt one-on-one with a guide. We had to walk the line. Act like we wanted a one-on-one, but then compromise to be put with others.

"But I was promised the best trophy opportunity there is. My daddy said—"

"Don't you worry about that. You'll get the hunt you want. I guarantee it."

Good start.

His guide service was absolutely legit, on the surface. Joe had booked a legal hunt, applied for licenses, et cetera, but he had long suspected Townsend of taking hunters inside the boundaries of the refuge or luring the record-sized bears out, which is illegal.

Townsend had proved to be sly over the years. No doubt, he'd have done his homework before taking us on as clients. Joe had painstakingly created backgrounds for us, complete with references from other shady trophy hunters, but we assumed Townsend would still need to feel us out. He'd dance around the subject at first, gauge our intent, in person, where nothing could be recorded or copied, before discussing an illegal hunt.

Once he did, that was only the first step. To be sure we could get a decent conviction, we had to witness the kill, then, if possible, mark the location. I had a camera with built-in

GPS, but DNA was an even stronger piece of evidence. If possible, we'd stash a piece of the carcass without the guide knowing. When the trophy got shipped to the lower forty-eight, crossing state lines, making it a clear violation of the Lacey Act (a federal law that prohibits trade in wildlife, fish, and plants that have been illegally taken, possessed, transported, or sold), then we'd have a solid case. We'd intercept at the change of hands and nail them both—guide and hunter.

"So we'll be camping backcountry, right, in a tent?" I gave him a whimpery smile, giving the impression I was uncomfortable with being alone in the wilderness.

He fiddled with the little wheel thing on the ceiling, looked over the gauges before he answered. "Depends."

"That's where the big bears are though, right? Deep in the woods."

"Honey," Joe piped up from the back seat. "Stop pestering Mark. Let the man do his job. I know you're excited, but we'll be there soon enough."

Joe'd been around long enough and had the confidence to know he didn't have to play it to the hilt. It was the little things that made a cover believable. He was a pro. I took his lead and crossed my arms and pursed my lips into a pout.

"See Mount Douglas?" Townsend pointed out the windshield, to the left. "We head that way, then to the right a bit. Not long. Sit back and relax. Enjoy the flight."

Right. I'd enjoy it a lot more if I knew how to fly this bird.

As we approached, I could see waves rippling across Iliamna Lake on the right, Mount Douglas up ahead, to the left. Townsend banked the plane and we started our descent. The lodge was somewhere to the southeast of Iliamna Lake, but north of the Katmai National Park and Preserve boundary, a swath of land larger than four million square acres.

Mark piped up again in his tour guide voice. "Katmai National Park was originally established because of the volcanic activity in the area known as The Valley of Ten Thousand Smokes."

He didn't mention that the protection of its brown bears has become equally vital. Most of the park is a designated wilderness area where hunting is banned. All wildlife is protected. Unfortunately, the bears don't live by the rule of boundaries. Nor do poachers, if they can cross over without getting caught.

"Over that way," he continued, gesturing out the window, "is the McNeil River. That's where the big boys hang out."

Famous among bear lovers, McNeil River Falls attracts the bruins in large numbers, the largest concentration of brown bears in the world, in fact. They gorge on the salmon that wiggle their way up from the sea, through the boulders and rocks, and try to jump the falls to continue upstream to their spawning grounds. Many of the bears have perfected catching the salmon in the air as they shoot out of the rapids. I've seen many pictures that were taken there. I'm told it's something to witness. I wished it was part of the tour.

Mark took us lower and flew along the coast before turning inland. The trees below showed the colors of autumn. Dark green spires of spruce popped up amid patches of yellow and gold with an occasional blot of reddish-orange. Trails cut through the alders and thicket, bear paths leading to and from the streams.

"Bears," came Joe's voice in my headset. "Off to the right."

I spun in my chair to see. A sow and her cub lumbered along a path, heading into the hills from the sea. I smiled. Wild and free. Beautiful.

"We're at the edge of the McNeil area. The lodge is just to the north. We'll be landing soon," Mark said and pushed the throttle forward. He'd just been showing us the goods.

Yep. We *so* had to bust this guy.

"Well, look at that," Mark said, leaning over to look out the side window.

I craned my neck on my side, trying to see what he saw.

He banked the plane to circle back. "The herd is moving."

Below, on the edge of a rocky slope, hundreds of caribou moved in unison, a river of shaggy coats. Their enormous antlers rocked to and fro as they ran. Caribou have the largest antlers relative to their body size among all deer species, and both male and female grow them. Running across the landscape, they looked like Santa's reindeer set free.

I watched them disappear over the hill as we flew onward.

Not ten minutes later, Mark turned the plane and lined up to touch down on a river. It felt like we were approaching at a pretty steep angle, but I didn't feel a deep descent.

"What's the trick to landing one of these?" I asked.

"No trick," he said. "They pretty much land themselves."

"How do you mean?"

He turned to me with a smirk. "What goes up must come down."

Right.

With Mark's experienced hand on the throttle, easing it back, the engine whir slowed and we simply glided right down to the water, smooth as can be.

I inhaled a deep breath. I love to fly, but there's always a sense of relief when I'm back on the ground. In this case, on the water.

We skidded along on the river's surface, then taxied to shore in front of the lodge, and pulled up next to another float plane. The propeller coughed and sputtered to a stop. We were here.

CHAPTER 4

After miles of pristine wilderness, the lodge stuck out like a festering scar on the face of the landscape. Tucked amid the pines, with the white mountains behind, its log walls and stone foundation matched the wilderness style, but its sheer size and modern shine seemed to spit at the idea of roughing it. I suppose it would appeal to an oil man from Oklahoma who was more interested in taking home a story than an actual wilderness experience.

A tall woman in a red flannel shirt waved from the porch, then came down to greet us, two Alaskan dogs at her heels. Close cousins to wolves, usually a mixed breed combining the best traits for sledding, with blue eyes, sharp noses, and thick coats, they looked like they had no problem keeping the bears at bay before curling up into a ball in front of the fireplace.

Townsend was out of the plane and securing it to a line before the woman got there. I climbed out onto the pontoon and leaped to the rocky shore where the two dogs greeted me with wet noses. Mark started shoving our bags out of the plane and the men lined up like in a bucket brigade, tossing the bags along, from one to the other to a pile on dry ground where a raven hopped about, his eye on the new arrivals.

The sky was such a vibrant shade of blue, it seemed to glow. Tall spruce lined the river. I drew in a deep breath. The air was so clean and fresh, as though one inhalation could cleanse my soul.

Feeling revitalized already, I knew I could handle anything that came my way on this op. And Stan Martin was thousands of miles away. Once we brought Townsend in, with everything by the book, he'd have to give me some credit. Dalton was right. I wasn't going to worry about it now. I'd focus on the op and deal with that later.

After the luggage was unloaded, Mark gestured toward the woman. "My wife, Irene." She stood at least a head taller than me, with a tiny frame, yet had the stature of someone who could haul half a moose cross-country, keeping up with Mark without breaking a sweat.

She acknowledged us with a warm smile. "Welcome to Moosepine Lodge. C'mon in. You're the last to arrive, so we'll get you settled, then make introductions." She glanced down at the pile of luggage, then me. "Which bag is yours, dear?"

I pointed to mine.

She hefted it over her shoulder and headed for the front door.

I let Dalton and Joe get the other bags. There were perks to playing the spoiled daughter.

Joe lumbered after Mark, but Dalton lingered, his eyes scanning the perimeter.

"Stop it," I whispered.

"What?"

"Stop acting like a SEAL. You're a farm boy from Oklahoma. Remember, the dopey older brother?"

"I know, Sis." He pointed at the treetops. "Look there. A bald eagle." The white-headed raptor circled in the sky. "Don't see them very often at home." He flashed his half-grin. My insides tingled. Damn. I had to figure out what to do about him. Yep. After this op, I needed some space to clear my head.

"Right," I said and spun around and followed Joe up the path, the crunch-crunch of stones beneath my feet.

Inside, Mark welcomed us with a grand gesture like we'd walked into Buckingham Palace.

Egads. Gaudy was an understatement. Cathedral ceilings rose high and spread wide to accommodate all the dead heads—moose, caribou, bear, dall sheep. Furs hung on the walls between the heads, draped on the back of the chairs, as rugs on the floor. The chandeliers were piles of antlers with tiny lights attached. The furniture was all brown leather and wood, lamps made of deer hooves and sheep horns.

The wood-plank floors stretched the length of the great room, to the fireplace on the other end, all stone to the ceiling, a giant moose head over the mantle. It was some kind of trophy hunter's live-in museum.

"Wow," I said, all bright eyed and impressed. *You like to kill things and show them off.*

Mark met my gaze. "You'll be leaving with your own, young lady," he said. "I guarantee it."

Irene still had my bag slung over her shoulder. "Show them to their room," she told Mark, then turned to me. "I'll take you to yours." To Joe and Dalton, she said, "And then if you will join us in the dining room, I'm just about to serve up some dinner."

"That sounds mighty fine," Joe said, rubbing his belly.

My room was small but quaint, in a hunter kind of way—deer hoof lamp, braided wool rug, red flannel bedspread. On the wall hung the head of a jackalope. Silly thing. A jackrabbit head mounted with antelope horns. Some kind of hunter's joke, a remnant of some hoax of the early 1800s. I wondered if I'd be able to sleep with its glass eyes staring at me.

Irene plopped my bag down on the bed. "It's nice to have another woman here to visit," she said. "Don't get that very often."

"I can imagine."

"Not many women from the lower forty-eights ever touch a

gun, let alone hunt. It's nice to see."

"Well, I guess you could say it's in my blood."

"Good," she said as she yanked the chain to turn on the deer-hoof lamp, then turned to me with a sadness in her expression. "Not many understand our way of life up here. Sometimes it's hand to mouth. We got to eat, ya know." There was an undertone to her voice that I couldn't quite figure out.

I nodded, not sure where this was coming from. Did she suspect me of being an agent and was she trying to play on my sympathy? Afraid for her way of life? Or was she simply a lonely woman looking for someone to talk to?

She managed a smile. "Though I suppose you're in it for the sport."

"I always liked guns as a girl. I suppose hunting was the natural thing to do next. But I admit," I said, returning a smile. "I've never had to hunt for my dinner."

"Yeah, I didn't think you did." She paused. "But that ain't the worst thing in the world." She sat down on the bed and let her shoulders slump as though this was the only break she'd have all day. "Take my advice, dear. Marry a nice young man with a degree in accounting. Or a doctor or dentist or something. Living off the land, well, it ain't all it's cracked up to be."

With the clients her husband had taken poaching, I couldn't imagine they were hurting for cash. Something didn't add up. Was it possible she didn't know? For a moment, I felt uncomfortable. My job was to go after the criminals, undercover, make friends, laugh with them, sometimes cry with them, then, when the moment presented itself, drag them off in handcuffs. They deserved justice, but still, with Irene, I felt a twinge of guilt. How would we know for sure if she was complicit?

She rose from the bed and moved toward the door, then turned and lingered in the doorway. "Well, like I said, it's nice to have you. And"—she jerked her head toward the window—"be careful out there."

"Thanks. I will," I said to her backside as she disappeared down the hall.

I sighed. *Damn.*

I quickly used the bathroom and headed to the dining room, anxious to meet the other hunters and guides.

Joe must have been thinking the same thing. He was already there, a glass of scotch in his hand.

Dalton stood beside him holding a bottle of Alaskan Ale. He looked so relaxed, at home, and so fricking sexy. I kept my eyes off of him, off that Navy-SEAL body ripped and hard in all the right places, and purposefully moved to meet the others.

There was no question who were the lodge staff and who were the hunters. Not just the clothes or physique, but there was something distinct about a true woodsman. "This is Jack," Mark said. "One of my best guides."

Jack nodded. Blue-eyed with a gentle smile, he must have been in his late twenties. He took my hand and gave it a squeeze. Nice guy.

"And that's Rocky," Mark said.

Rocky leaned against the dining table, his hands gripping the edge. I couldn't see his eyes. It was as though he purposefully hid them under the shadow of his ball cap. Lanky and awkward, he reminded me of a boy I'd gone to high school with. On graduation day, he'd told me he'd tried a hundred times to ask me out. I felt like a real snob because I didn't even know his name. Billy, maybe?

Rocky touched his greasy hat and muttered, " 'lo."

"He's also the mechanic around here," Mark added.

Something about him struck me as one of those people who were drawn to the wilderness of Alaska to get away from life in the lower forty-eight. Most times, they were running from something.

"You're practically neighbors," Mark said.

Alarms went off in my brain, bringing me fully alert. "Neighbors?"

"You're from Mississippi, ain't ya?" he said to Rocky.

Rocky gave a hint of a nod, staring at me with flat, unblinking eyes.

"You ride rodeo?" I asked, hoping he didn't.

"Nope," he muttered without moving a muscle. His eyes dropped to the floor.

Irene came through the door from the kitchen, saving me from the awkward conversation. She wore a starched white apron wrapped around her waist and carried a tray in her hand loaded with mystery meat chunks stabbed with toothpicks. She plopped it down on the table.

"What can I get you to drink, dear?" she asked me.

"Wine?"

She hesitated, eyebrows raised.

Oops. What is the drinking age in Oklahoma? Or Alaska for that matter? "My daddy lets me drink one glass when we're on vacation."

She nodded and disappeared without asking white or red. *Yep. I was getting White Zinfandel.* My penchant for wine wasn't going to be relevant here anyway.

Mark gestured toward us, addressing everyone else in the room. "This is Joe. His son, Dalton. And his daughter, Penelope."

"Everyone calls me Poppy," I said. We'd agreed that Poppy was such an uncommon name that it made the most sense to use it like a nickname when undercover. The last thing I needed was someone outing me by Googling my name.

Mark continued the introductions, turning to two men who appeared as though they'd just stepped from the check-out lane at Cabela's. Obviously brothers. They had the same rounded jaws, same pencil-thin necks, same pompous posture. East coast, Ivy League bred. In their late forties or early fifties. Eyes zeroing in on me like a couple of jackals. "And these are long time friends of mine, John and Patrick."

We all shook hands. True to form, Mark purposefully didn't share last names. No matter. We'd find them all later. Right now, our job was to make friends, get invited to hunt with them so we could witness the poaching act.

Dalton struck up a conversation easily with Patrick whose eyes lingered on me.

John made the move toward me with a grin, showing his perfect teeth. He'd obviously already had a few drinks. "Mark tells me you're here on your own hunt." His eyes lingered on my chest before slowly making their way back up. *Eyes up here, buddy.* "I wasn't expecting to meet Annie Oakley on the trip."

Was that supposed to be a compliment? Excuse me, there's still a price tag hanging on your jacket. Dope. "Oh, yeah," I said. "I've been Crawford County's Little Miss Sharpshooter champ since I was, like, three."

"No kidding," he said, his eyes alight as if I'd just told him I was a champion pole dancer.

"Daddy's been, like, promising to take me on a big hunt for since, like, as long as I can remember." I grinned with delight. "I can't wait."

"Oh honey, it's a rush like nothing else you could imagine."

His eyes dropped to my chest again. *Lech.*

"At least with your clothes on," he added.

Okay, that was enough. "You know, in Oklahoma, we have a saying—"

"Poppy," said Dalton, moving between John and me, "be a good sis and get me another beer." He shoved his empty bottle in my hand.

I shoved it back. "Get your own."

"Ooh, red hot and sassy," John tittered.

But Dalton had accomplished what he wanted and kept his place between us, establishing himself as the protective older brother. It was all about roles, playing off your partner's improv. You could always work it to your advantage. At least that's what Joe had taught me.

I grinned at John like I'd like to meet him out back later. That ought to keep him interested.

Already enjoying the hors d'oeuvres were a group of five men, foreigners I was sure. Russian. Maybe German. All in their fifties or older with the bellies of serious beer drinkers.

They were nodding and smiling, but I could tell they weren't sure of the content of our conversation. One of the five made eye contact with me and, with a respectful nod, said, "'Tis nice to meet you."

"You too," I said. "Where are you from?"

"East Germany," he said. "I speak little of the English. My friends, not so much."

"I see," I said. I speak some German, learned it when my mom was briefly stationed in Germany, and maybe it would get me invited to hunt with them, but my gut told me that right now, it would be best to keep that a secret, see what I could pick up.

Irene appeared and gave me a wink as she handed me a glass filled to the rim with pink wine. I thanked her and turned back to my German friend.

John hovered at my shoulder, whispered in my ear, "Ask him if he's a communist."

"So are you here to fish and hunt?" I asked.

"Here, in America?" John added.

The four other men wore the expressions of those lost in a maze, curiously trying to find their way.

"Fish, some, yes," he said. "Hunt, some."

"Of course," John muttered.

"Bear?" I asked.

"Bear. Yes. Big bear." He raised his arms like a bear standing on his hind legs. The other men grinned and nodded.

"Yes, big bear," I said.

"Oh Jesus," John said and turned away.

"Well, good luck." I held up my glass and produced the only phrase a red-blooded, American girl from Oklahoma would be likely to know, "Nasdrovia."

Instantly, all five men came alive, raising their glasses and simultaneously cheering, "Nasdrovia!" followed by chuckles and happy chatter.

Joe eased next to me. "It seems you're making friends, my dear."

"It seems so."

"Joe tells me this is your very first big game hunt," Townsend said. "I didn't realize."

"And nothing but the best will do for my little angel," Joe said. "I hope you've got something real special planned for her."

I nodded and grinned like an idiot. "I'm so excited." I took Joe's hand and leaned into him, a daughter affectionately snuggling up to her dad. "I can't believe I'll be hunting tomorrow already."

"Not so fast, young lady. You'll have to wait one more day," Joe said.

I frowned at Joe and looked back to Townsend. "I don't understand."

"Tomorrow, we sight in the rifles," he answered. "I'll be assessing your skills and discussing with each of you what you want from the hunt. Then I'll determine where we'll go. Some of our spike camps are quite remote." He winked. "I want to make sure you're up to it."

"You mean you want to make sure I'm not some frou-frou

girl who doesn't know which end of the rifle to aim at the target."

He grinned. "Something like that."

"Well," I said. "We'll see you tomorrow then."

Everyone retired to their rooms, anxious for the next day to begin. Being the only female guest, I had my own room, but we still shared bathrooms. After brushing my teeth, heading back down the hall to my room, I heard voices, a conversation in German. I paused outside the door, listening, ready to bolt at any moment.

„Er hat mir einen Bären als Trophäe versprochen versprochen. Ich komme seit drei Jahren hierher. Ich habe dafür bezahlt und dann bekomme ich das auch." *He's promised me a trophy bear. For three years I've been coming here. That's what I paid for, that's what I'm going to get.*

„Und er soll verdammt nochmal auch mit uns rauskommen und nicht einmal daran denken, uns mit irgend so einem Typen, den er angeheuert hat, loszuschicken. Oder wird sind hier fertig." *And he damn well better take us out himself, not send us with some hired man. Or we're done.* Something like that. My German was rusty.

„Da bin ich ganz deiner Meinung." *I agree.* I recognized the voice of the one I'd spoken to at dinner. „Ich werde ihm sagen, was ihr wollt." *I will tell him our demands.*

„Und ich gehe auch nicht mit diesem verwöhnten kleinen Mädchen auf die Jagd." *I'm not going out with that spoiled little rich girl either.* A new voice.

I frowned. Maybe I'd overdone it. If they got their way, and Mark took them out hunting himself, without at least one of the three of us, we'd be here for nothing.

„Ich hatte schon mit Frauen wie ihr zu tun. Pfff. Amerikanerinnen." *Pfff. Americans. I've had to deal with women like her before.*

„Alles klar" said the leader. *I understand.* „Ich spreche gleich morgen früh mit ihm." *I'll tell him first thing in the morning.*

The door flew open. I jumped back with a start, dropping my toothbrush. It skittered across the hardwood floor.

The German hesitated, suspicion in his eyes.

"Omigosh, you startled me," I said, gripping the front of my robe to hold it closed. "I thought everyone had gone to bed already."

The one who spoke English poked his head through the door. "So sorry, my lady."

"It's all right," I said. "No harm done." I flashed him a grin. "Got my heart going though." I added a giggle.

"Yah, yah. Good thing not a bear in da woods, no?"

I nodded and giggled some more.

The first man picked up my toothbrush and handed it to me.

"You will need to keep better grip on your gun, I am thinking."

"Yes, yes, I will," I said, all girly embarrassment. *Jerk.*

I slinked back to my room. *Damn.* My chances of hunting with them were nil. Joe would have to make that connection. I was left with the chest-ogling Lech Brothers if I was going to be successful.

CHAPTER 5

Sourdough pancakes dripping with boysenberry syrup, reindeer sausage the size of my arm and a heap of scrambled eggs covered my breakfast plate. My eyes must have revealed my overwhelmed appetite.

"Everything's big in Alaska," Mark said. "Eat up. We've got a busy day planned."

Dalton, playing up the annoying big brother, stabbed my sausage with his fork and dragged it over to his plate.

"Hey!" I said, secretly thanking him.

"Eat your eggs, then maybe you can have some more," he said with a smirk.

After the plates were cleared, Mark instructed us to bring our rifles from our rooms and we headed to a clearing behind the lodge, the two dogs following us as if they were our guards, keeping the wild things at bay. The shooting range had been set up with sighting benches on one end, targets on the other.

The Germans went to work right away, loading rounds into guns the size of shoulder-fired rocket launchers and pacing the distance to their targets. All business.

The Lech brothers hung back, more interested in watching me than getting their own weapons ready. I smiled and nodded, acting like I enjoyed the attention.

They were my target, our best shot at catching Townsend. The tricky part would be proving a monetary transaction occurred between them and Townsend. But we could make a case with the assumption. The odds were good that once we threatened them with jail time, they'd flip on Townsend. Fine by us. It was Townsend we were after.

Today was my chance to form the relationship.

Rocky came up to me. "You need any help?" he asked without making eye contact.

"Nope, all set," I said. "Old hat."

He nodded but with a hesitation, as though he were disappointed, then moved on to check with the Germans.

Dalton set the gun case on the bench and I removed my rifle, a brand new Ruger 375 H&H Mag, single-shot. Story was, Daddy Pratt had bought it for me, special for this trip. I dropped a single round into the chamber, then snapped it shut.

"Now for the show," I whispered to Dalton.

"Easy, Sis," he muttered.

I got myself situated on the sight bench and took a couple deep breaths. I hadn't done this in a while, but I wasn't worried. I'd won the firearm medal back in training. I knew how to obliterate a target.

When Mark hollered all clear, I lined up the crosshairs, inhaled, then on my exhale, gently eased my finger back on the trigger and fired a round. The butt kicked against my shoulder. I looked down the sights to confirm. Right smack in the bullseye, dead center. *Shazam! I rock.*

I cracked the barrel to spring the empty shell, then loaded another round and did it again. Then again. Three right in the eye.

"Hold your fire," Mark yelled.

Joe held the binoculars up to his eyes. "That's my girl!"

"Impressive," said John the lech, his eyes all heavy. *What is it with these men?* "What you got there? Some kind of canon?"

I held it up for him to examine, all proud. "This here's the finest in bear-huntin' weaponry." With a wink, I added, "Don't you go droolin' on it, now."

He ran his hand down the barrel. "That she is. Single-shot, eh?"

Single-shot weapons were an ego thing with big hunters. "When you only have one shot, make it count," I said, rattling off the company slogan.

"Well, aren't you something."

Part of me thought I should drive it home, ask to see his gun, play up the sexual innuendo. But like Joe had taught me, sometimes less is more. I took the rifle from his hands, passed it to Dalton with a two-handed toss, John Wayne-style, then jerked my thumb toward the bullseye. "Beat that score, Brother," I said and strutted downrange to put up a new target, knowing John watched my backside as I went.

Mark sauntered up to me, Rocky behind him like a shadow. "Nice shootin' Tex."

"Well, yeah, except I'm from Oklahoma."

"Right," he said, giving me a nod of respect. "I forgot." He stuck his finger in the hole my bullets had left in the paper bullseye. "You put all three in the center. But can you do it to a bear?" His eyes locked onto me. "When you got yourself all in a froth of excitement?"

Froth of excitement? Seriously? "I didn't start shooting yesterday."

"Shooting, yeah. But when a bear is charging, bearing down on you, and adrenaline is pumping through your veins, your heart hammerin' away in your chest, will Little Miss Sharpshooter hold that gun steady then?"

I eyed him, trying to get a read on him. Rocky hovered at his shoulder, standing at attention like a soldier, ready to serve.

"You make it sound like in the movies," I said.

"That's what you're here for, ain't ya?" Mark said with a sly grin. "The thrill? Like in the movies."

I looked from Rocky to Mark and held his stare. *Was that his pitch?* "Well, yeah," I said with a little too much smartass.

"Bear hunting isn't for light-weights with soft hearts," Mark said, taking a step closer to me. "You gotta be fierce."

"I'm fierce."

Rocky closed in on Mark's flank.

"Sometimes, shit happens," Mark said. "You've gotta be able to roll with it."

"I can roll."

Mark looked me up and down as though assessing my level of fortitude. I stared right back at him. "There are some mean, crafty beasts out there."

Rocky added, his tone matter-of-fact, "Rip yer pretty little head off with a single swipe of the paw."

I put my hands on my hips. "Are you trying to scare me? Cuz it ain't working. I'm not some little girl afraid of breaking a nail. I'm taking home a bear. The bigger the better." I glanced back toward Joe, who was watching every move without giving up that he was watching. "And I want a story to go with it."

Mark's lip curled up into a grin. "All right, little lady. I just might have the right one for you. One I've had my eye on. He's a mean old bear. He won't be taken easily. It will be extra work and the added danger—"

"No problem." I gave him my high-and-mighty-princess face. "My daddy will pay."

After cleaning our weapons and packing our gear for the backcountry, we were served a lunch, the portions sized for lumberjacks, during which I managed the art of keeping John and his brother Patrick interested with hunting tales laced

with eyelash batting and winks. Then Mark took us all for a
pontoon boat ride down the river.

I tuned out the hum of the engine and took in the scenery
around me, the vast, awe-inspiring Alaskan landscape—a
shoreline strewn with round rocks, tumbled smooth over eons
of ice movement, granite hills at the river's edge clad with
dark green forest, evergreens overhanging a dense understory
of alder and devil's club, that thorny weed with giant leaves
that's the bane of any hiker. A gentle mist hung amid the trees,
a white swath, like cotton stretched across the treetops.

Eagles perched at regular intervals on the river, each
claiming a territory. As we motored by, one lifted on his
haunches and tipped forward, swooping from his branch, his
great wings outstretched into a gentle glide toward the river's
surface. Then in an instant, he changed the angle of his wings,
thrust his talons forward, and snatched a fish from the water.
With three powerful flaps of his wings, he headed skyward
again, back to his perch, his meal pierced by his talons.

The men didn't say much as we motored down the river for
several miles then finally came to a sandy spit. Mark drove the
pontoons right up on shore and killed the engine.

"A short walk, my friends," he said as he got up from the
driver's seat. He clipped a large can of pepper spray onto his
belt, said, "Let's stay together," and led the way.

Seagulls scattered and took flight as the group walked
down the shoreline, then up and over a ridge. Before us, a
wide stream narrowed to a spot where the water tumbled over
rocks into a natural pool, a place for salmon to gather before
launching themselves into the air, hoping to clear the rocky
barrier.

Three bears waded belly deep, their heads down, searching
for fish. One saw something and pounced, the splash causing
a wave to ripple across the pool. His entire head went
underwater, but he came up empty, droplets of water clinging

to his fur.

"Let's keep our distance," Mark said, holding up a hand, gesturing for us to stay put. "This is a good spot to watch."

"Looks like a good spot to hunt," said Patrick, crossing his arms.

"Nah. The big boys have moved on. These are the stragglers, picking off the last of the salmon. Just thought you might enjoy a little viewing. A preview, if you will."

There was a rustle in the bushes above the falls. A bear with fur the color of amber poked her head out, then ambled toward the stream. Two spring cubs followed.

I fought to contain a smile as my insides tingled with delight.

The sow scanned the area, alert for trouble. Her eyes sparkled with intelligence. She was a big bear, bigger than the three in the pool, which were likely adolescents. I'd guess six hundred pounds. If she had raised up on her hind legs, I'd guess she stood eight feet tall.

She lumbered down the edge of the stream, taking her time, and as she entered the water, just above the falls, the three young bears hightailed it for the woods. There was no confrontation, no growling, no threat. Just the hierarchy of the animal kingdom. She was a bigger bear. It was her turn at the table.

Her cubs stayed at the edge of the water, watching their mother, their innocent brown eyes taking it all in.

"That's a nice size one," John said to Mark, as if to prove him wrong.

His brother elbowed him. "She's got cubs, man."

It's illegal to take a sow with cubs, not to mention downright immoral. I harbored hope that even poachers wouldn't cross that line. Roy, the weathered old agent I was assigned to during my probationary training always said, "You can hope in one hand and shit in the other. What have you got?" Pretty much sums it up.

The sow's movements were slow and deliberate. No energy wasted. She had a long winter ahead and needed every pound of stored fat. So did her cubs. And feeding them was a big chore; they weren't worried about conserving energy. The two wrestled and tumbled, romping around in circles, their awkward little legs moving them about. Round a tree stump they chased, one, then the other, changing direction. Mom glanced in their direction, a tolerant expression on her face.

I wanted to pick one up and cuddle it. They were so cute, all fluffy fur and pink bellies. Those little round ears must be so soft. But if I even got close, it'd be the last thing I ever did. Mother bears were notoriously protective of their cubs. If she wanted to, she'd be on me within seconds. One swipe of her massive paw could rip my guts open. Rocky was right about that.

"Still," John muttered. "That rug would look damn good in front of my fireplace."

Patrick gave him a conspiratorial grin.

"And some little rugs in my den," John muttered.

My throat burned with acid. His arrogance was astounding, not to mention his lack of ethics. All he could think about was killing, yet the bear was the one with the reputation of being a vicious killer. The bear stood not forty yards away, a distance she could cover in seconds, yet hadn't given him a second look. She had no cause. We weren't overtly threatening her or her cubs. For her, like all wild animals, fighting is a dangerous business. One doesn't pick a fight without good reason.

The mama bear swatted her paw in the water, trying to stun a fish. She reared back and plunged in, coming up with a wriggling salmon in her mouth.

She plodded to the shore and plopped down, the salmon fighting a hopeless battle in her powerful jaws. She clamped her mighty paws around the fish and with her teeth, gripped it in the middle and ripped its skin off, all the way to the tail, revealing its pink flesh. The cubs circled round, whimpering for a bite.

Three gulls swooped in and danced about, squawking, trying to get a tidbit for themselves. The bear ripped off a mouthful, chewed sloppily as she kept a wary eye on her surroundings, always alert, then swallowed the precious protein and tore off another bite.

When the fish was gone, she waded into the pool again, milled around for some time, but found nothing. It was late in the year. Most of the salmon were gone. She gave up and hauled out, water pouring off of her, then shook, water spraying every which way.

At the river's edge, she lay down in the grass, rolled over on her back, and let her cubs crawl atop her to nurse.

I couldn't keep the smile from tugging at the corners of my mouth. I wanted to giggle with joy in seeing these bears, right in front of me, in their natural habitat, doing what bears do. I felt such wonder. I wanted to share it with Dalton, tell him about the awe I felt. But right now, my goal was to be someone else. Someone who didn't care. Someone who only wanted to kill, to own, to conquer.

"We should have brought our guns," I said and crossed my arms, like a bored, rich, gun-toting cowgirl.

Back at the dock, Rocky helped catch the pontoon boat and tie it up. Mark pulled Joe, Dalton and me aside while the other guests filed into the lodge. Rocky lingered behind him.

Mark addressed me. "We've talked and made a plan. Rocky has had his eye on a bear he thinks is just right for you. He's set up a spike camp in the area. He'll fly you out there." He looked to Dalton, then back to me. "Your brother here can go, too. Back you up with that fancy single-shot rifle." He cuffed me on the chin as if I were thirteen. "Just in case you're all bark and no bite."

I pushed out my lower lip. "Rocky? I thought you were the legend, the man to hunt with." I couldn't let him send me out with his sidekick. If that happened, the op would be over for me.

"Well, I wish I could take every client on every hunt, but I can't be everywhere at once, now can I? Trust me. Rocky here will take real good care of you."

This was my last chance. I had to be on the hunt with Mark. This was the moment. All or nothing. I needed to throw a class-A fit.

I glared at him, forcing my lips into a frown. "Seriously? This guy?" I said, jerking my thumb toward Rocky. "You said fierce. He doesn't look that fierce." I rammed my fists into my hips. "Give me a rope, I'll drop him on his ass." I turned to Joe. "Daddy, you told me I was gonna get the best. I don't wanna go out with this—" I flicked a dismissive hand in the air "—this clown. He doesn't even look like he's smart enough to come in outta the rain."

"It's all right, Poppy," Joe soothed. He turned to Mark, playing along. "Can't we work something out? If it's the cost—"

Mark held up a conciliatory hand. "Now, I understand your reservations. But trust me when I say, Rocky's my best guide." Rocky's eyes never left the ground. "He's got the highest kill rate of any I've ever worked with. You want to take home a trophy, he's your man." He slapped Joe on the back at the shoulder. "I know how it is. Everyone wants to go out with the owner. But believe me when I say, I only hire the best. That's how I built my reputation. When you come to Moosepine Lodge, you go home with a trophy." He rocked back on his heels, a smug smile on his face, satisfied that he'd been convincing. "Rocky's been scouting all summer. He's got his sights on the one for her. I'm telling you. Guaranteed. Your little lady won't be disappointed."

"But Daddy, you said—"

The look on Joe's face silenced me. Better to back off than blow it. You can always come around for a second shot at 'em if you keep the cover intact.

Maybe we'd been overly optimistic to think that the first time around Mark would take us out hunting himself. We'd have to play the game, bide our time, and book another trip next year. It made me want to scream bloody murder to let it ride for that long, but it was how the game was played.

I crossed my arms, filled with disappointment. "Fine."

After dinner and the obligatory cocktails and all the pomp of huntsmen's well wishes, we retired to our rooms. The plan was to meet in Joe and Dalton's room for a strategic discussion and update.

I took my time washing my face and doing some stretching before sneaking across the hall. Dalton was leaning against the dresser in his casual way, his hair ruffled. *Damn. Why does he have to be so good looking?*

Joe sat down on the leather chair, always professional and serious. "So. This is how it is. He's sending the two of you out with Rocky. The brothers are going together with someone named Bob." He threw his hands up with a shrug. We hadn't met anyone named Bob. "Maybe someone flying in? Anyway, Townsend's taking the Germans out himself. I'll be hunting with Jack. I tried to get him to combine the two groups, insisting I didn't need one guide to myself, since he'll have all five of the Germans, but he said he'd take his wife. He's smart. He's giving us the VIP treatment while simultaneously creating a situation with no witnesses for corroboration. Makes it awfully hard to nail him for poaching."

"Okay, but what if Rocky or Jack takes one of us inside the park boundary?" I asked, grabbing for anything. "Can't we cite Mark for knowingly promoting illegal hunting? I mean, he's the boss here."

"Doesn't matter," Joe said. "If an undercover agent acts as the hunter and makes the kill, they could claim entrapment. It wouldn't be worth it. It'd be a slap on the wrist anyway. When we nail this guy, I want rock-hard evidence."

"So we're stuck here in an our-word-against-his scenario?"

Joe nodded. "We'll have to play along, keep the cover, see if an opportunity arises."

"And if it doesn't?"

"Try again next year," he said with the matter-of-fact tone of many years of experience.

"But we've come all this way."

"I'm glad he's sending me with you," Dalton said to me. "There's something about Rocky. I don't like him."

"This sucks," I said, unable to contain my frustration. "Maybe I could talk to John and Patrick—"

"We don't want to push too hard and blow it," Joe said. "Stay the course."

I nodded. He was the boss. I'd go with Rocky and play along. *But that means—*My heart started to race and my stomach turned sour.

Dalton moved to within my gaze. "Poppy, if you're not sure—"

"I understand."

A look passed between him and Joe.

"I understand my job." I turned toward the door. "I'll be ready. See you in the morning." I needed some air, some space. I went straight down the stairs and out the front door into the dark night.

I pulled my jacket up around my neck and crossed my arms, snugging it tight. I wasn't to the dock yet when I heard footsteps behind me. Dalton.

"You okay?"

"Fine. I just needed some fresh air."

"Let's walk," he said and took me by the arm.

About forty yards down the shoreline, he turned to me and whispered, "Are you ready for this?"

"I said I was." *This again.* "I understand the situation. For now, we play the game. And someday we'll nail these guys. Somehow. Some way."

He nodded and stood in silence for a time, his eyes on me. I couldn't meet his gaze. He'd been trying to warn me. It was going to be just like he'd said.

We walked a little further.

"Could you believe John and Patrick today?" I said. "I wanted to smack their heads together and drop them on their asses." I turned to face him. "You know what I'm going to do? When we do finally bust Townsend, I hope those two go down with him. I hope they make a plea deal. I'll petition the judge to require community service from them.

"I want to see John standing in front of a school group, his ranger hat in his hand, telling the kids, 'Bears aren't vicious, savage beasts that stalk and kill humans like you might think. They're highly intelligent beings. Surely smarter than I am.'

"Yeah, I'm going to ask the judge to let me write their whole script. His brother will stand beside him. 'Humans aren't on the menu,' he'll say. 'But if a bear feels threatened, he'll defend himself, and then make a meal out of the kill. That's nature at work. The circle of life. The balance of prey and predator. The way it's supposed to be.' I'll make sure the judge requires that last line. Every time. 'The way it's supposed to be.'"

"Poppy?"

"I know." I plopped down on the rocks and pulled my knees up to my chest. "I know." I swallowed and drew in a breath. "You're assuming Rocky will even bring in a bear. The odds are—"

"The odds are good. He's a poacher. He'll do anything it takes. There's big money at stake."

I nodded, resigned. He wasn't telling me anything I didn't know. "God it's beautiful here. Look how the stars fill the sky like glitter sprinkled across black velvet." He stared at me. "I love how the air smells. Like fall, all earthy and wet. And listen to the river gurgle at the edges where it laps on the gravel. It's like music—"

"I know how you feel about this. And if we need to—"

"No, you don't," I said, too sharply. "You don't know how I feel about it."

He set his jaw, holding back. "Fine. But I do know that one mistake could get us killed." He paused and I could tell he was carefully planning his words. "And I don't like going in with a partner I'm not sure I can trust to do what needs to be done."

My heart rate shot up. "I told you. I'll do my job."

"I don't question your dedication. Or your abilities," he said through clenched teeth. "I need to know that you're gonna pull the goddamn trigger."

He stared at me. I bit my lip, staring back.

"I'm your partner. I've got your back. But—" He pressed his lips together.

I opened my mouth to answer, but I couldn't. I didn't have one.

"Poppy, listen to me. It's not going to be like you said about the trophy mount in the airport, you looking through the sights at some cuddly, sleeping bear. He'll probably provoke it. And the question is, when that bear is charging right at you, are you set in your mind to pull the trigger?" He moved so I was looking him in the eye. "I know you. You tell yourself that you wouldn't. You might even believe you wouldn't. But when it happens, when you are facing the reality, when it comes down to that life or death moment, I think you will."

What? I jerked back. "Are you saying I'm really a killer at heart?"

"I'm saying you've never stared death in the face. And," he paused, "you don't know how devastating it can be."

"Now you're confusing me. Are you worried I won't do my job, or worried that when I do, it will break my heart?"

"Both." He sighed. "I'm trying to tell you that you need to decide right now. You need to be ready. You need to have that set in your mind. Because in that moment, when that animal's bearing down on you, if you even hesitate—"

"I get it!"

He shook his head, exhaling with a huff. "I don't think you do."

"Oh, I do. You don't have to say it for the twenty-seventh time. You don't like working with me. Fine. When we get back, I'll probably be demoted or fired or whatever anyway and you'll get your wish."

"What?" He pulled back. "That's not true."

"You don't like my approach. You don't like my views. You're afraid that—"

"Yes, Poppy, I'm afraid. I'm afraid your idealism is going to get you killed."

I drew back. That stung. I closed my eyes and calmly said, "Please leave me alone. Go back to the lodge. And leave me alone."

"Not a good idea." A voice behind us. We both spun around. It was Rocky. *Crap.* How long had he been there? He stood ten paces away. A shadow in the night. "You shouldn't be out here at night. You never know what might be lurking in them woods."

Or who?

"Right," Dalton said. "We were just heading back in."

CHAPTER 6

The air had turned moist overnight and a hint of fog hung in the shadows. Like a scene from a postcard, the sun rose over the hills and bathed the forest in a misty crimson and ochre. Tiny specks of sunlight sparkled on the river.

Without a word, Rocky loaded our gear into the back of the plane, the same plane we'd flown in on with Mark. We were headed out to the spike camp for seven to ten days to find a trophy-sized bruin, a bear for the record books. No other details were given, of course. We were to smile and nod and put all our faith into the guide. That's how it works. There's no actual hunting involved. They serve up a trophy on a silver platter. All we needed to do was actually pull the trigger.

Irene emerged from the lodge, waving for us to wait, a canvas bag in her other hand. "Lunch for the flight out," she said and handed me the bag with a genuine smile. Her hand lingered, holding mine for a moment. With a determined gaze, she said, "Be careful." I thanked her with a smile.

Once again, I climbed into the passenger seat, making Dalton sit in the back. I wasn't in the mood to sit next to him.

If we couldn't go out with Townsend, why couldn't we have gotten assigned with cute Jack? He seemed kind, personable even. Or the mysterious Bob. Rocky went about his work without notice that actual humans were part of the equation. He kept his head down, didn't make eye contact.

Maybe I'd gone too far with my dismissal of him and he'd taken it personally and felt insulted. I *had* called him a clown. I'm sure they'd dealt with arrogant clients before, though. Oh well. There was nothing to do about it now.

Rocky climbed into the pilot seat.

"Good morning," I said, trying to lighten the mood.

He paused, looking ahead as though he might turn to stone if he dared to look me in the eye. "Mornin'." He went through all the motions, flipping switches, pumping levers, and the propeller started spinning. "Buckle your seatbelt. The weather's supposed to turn. It'll be a rough flight," he said, an edge to his voice, more threat than warning.

Well, I guess that answers that question.

He scanned and rescanned the dashboard. Not like Mark had done, checking and double checking all the controls. Rocky seemed impatient, like waiting for the engine to warm up created an unbearable time gap of inaction.

"Is something wrong?" I asked. "With the plane?"

He turned to me, his gaze a gray stare. "Don't you worry your pretty little head. I'm quite capable."

Something about his stare made me back down. "That's not what I meant," I said. The last thing I wanted to do was insult the guy any further. "I just, you know, don't like flying." That was a good lie.

He pushed the throttle lever forward, the engine fired up, and we were in motion. He turned his steel gray eyes on me again. "Everything will be all right. You're with me now. I'll take good care of you."

Somehow that didn't feel comforting.

The rain came while in flight. Water droplets hit the windshield and slid off leaving tiny trails, making the view muted and blurry. The whir of the engine and the steamy warmth inside the cockpit pushed me into a drowsy state.

We flew south-southwest. Right toward the park. We'd either be within the boundary, which was illegal, and risky with a plane, which was easily seen, or, more likely, just outside of it, to lure a bear out of the refuge.

And there was nothing we could do about it.

Rocky pulled back on the throttle and we started to descend toward a small lake tucked in among what appeared to be rolling hills, but I was coming to realize that what they said was true: everything's big in Alaska. The landscape was so vast, it was hard to judge distance and size. Those hills were probably considered mountains back home.

He banked the plane sharply, dipping hard to the right, then made a full circle as he descended, scanning the surface of the lake for any obstructions before touching down.

We taxied to shore, leaving a ripple that slowly crossed the silvery water, disrupting the perfect reflection of the birches and diamond willows that grew at the water's edge.

Two ravens swooped down, landed on the shore, then hippety-hopped along toward us as if in greeting.

Rocky left the engine running while he and Dalton unloaded all our gear, then took off his raincoat, then his shirt and boots, and threw them onto the pile, then waded into the water, pushing the plane out from shore.

"What's going on?" I asked.

"Wait here," he said and climbed into the cockpit.

"What's he doing?" I asked Dalton.

Dalton was scanning the hillside. "I assume he wants the plane where he can see it."

"What's he so paranoid about?"

He shrugged. "Beats me."

I wore a rain hat and rain coat, but the rain was really coming down, cold and misty. Fall in Alaska. Fog enveloped the forest, but hints of treetops poked through on the hillside. I pulled my coat closer, slid my gloved hands into the pockets.

Dalton turned to me. "Hey, listen about last night—"

"Forget it," I said. "Let's just do this thing and go home."

I snugged my coat up closer around my neck.

Dalton looked away. "Hey, look at that."

A blur of brown feathers dropped from the sky—an eagle, its feet stretched out beneath, talons ready to grip. Below, a squirrel darted behind a rock. The eagle arched its powerful wings, slowing its descent, just as the squirrel burrowed in, but its tail was still hanging out, vulnerable. The eagle snatched ahold and flapped, once, twice, and lifted into the air again, the squirrel dangling in its grasp.

The squirrel let out a shriek and twisted and dropped to the rocks below. With a flip, it was running again for a larger rock to hide behind and hunkered down.

The eagle, trying to change direction at such low altitude, fluttered and spun before landing, its sharp eyes fixed on the location of the squirrel.

The squirrel made a run for it. I winced. *You were safe where you were!*

With a whoosh of his enormous wings, the eagle lifted and pounced, this time snatching up the squirrel about the belly. He didn't have a chance. His little feet swayed, lifeless in the eagle's grasp as it flapped hard to get airborne again, then flew back to its perch among the treetops.

An incredible silence descended on us. Rocky had set an anchor and cut the engine. The sounds of the forest—the glock-glock of a raven in the distance, the patter of raindrops hitting leaves—were all enveloping, like being wrapped in a blanket of nature.

We turned toward the lake and watched Rocky swim back to the gravel beach.

"That water is ice cold," I said as he trudged over the pebbled shoreline in bare feet, water sloshing down his camo pants.

"It's okay," he said through clenched teeth, then paused long enough to look me right in the eyes. "I'm fierce. Really. You'll see."

Dalton and I exchanged a glance. *Uh...weird.*

He put his shirt back on, slid his raincoat and boots on, slung his duffle bag over his shoulder, his rifle case strapped to it, then from a canvas bag, he pulled out a modern, compact crossbow outfitted with a hefty scope. It looked like something The Green Arrow would carry.

"Sweet," Dalton said, admiring the weapon. "Is that the new Carbon Express?"

Rocky nodded, barely acknowledging Dalton.

"You use carbon fiber arrows?"

Rocky ignored him altogether.

"Whew," Dalton continued anyway. "That thing is accurate as hell. Dude, you could put one right between a bear's eyes."

Rocky paused, looked at Dalton, resigned, as though dealing with him pushed Rocky to the edge of his patience. "Ptarmigan. For dinner," he said, annoyed. "We don't need to draw any unwanted attention firing a gun."

"You're going to shoot birds with that?" Dalton said with awe.

Ptarmigan are large grouse that provide an exciting challenge for hunters. They lift off abruptly and fly erratically.

Rocky turned to me. "Let's go," he said and took off, pushing through the alder-brush like he had something to prove.

Suddenly I was glad Dalton was with me. He was right. Something was off about this guy.

I hefted my backpack. "I guess we follow him."

Rocky led us through the thick tangle of alders that lined the lake, branches scrapping at my jacket and snagging at every seam, until finally we emerged in a forest of old growth trees. The terrain reminded me in some ways of the steamy jungle in the Philippines, though the temperature here was seventy degrees cooler. Beneath the dark canopy of spruce and juniper, willow and birch, the rain still found a way in.

We slowly made our way over deadfall covered in moss and slick with water, pushing through blueberry bushes and devil's club and many kinds of ferns, the rain pitter-pattering on my hat, drowning out the sounds of the forest.

It was rough going with the heavy pack, but Rocky never slowed, never even looked back. Usually, I wouldn't bother to try to keep up. Pacing is important and being in the elements, especially rain, presents risks that otherwise wouldn't be an issue. If I hiked too fast and got sweaty underneath my raincoat, I'd get cold later when I stopped. If I unzipped my coat so I wouldn't get too warm, I'd get wet anyway from the rain.

But today, I didn't want to lose sight of Rocky. So we climbed upward at a pace that, I admit, made me winded. Dalton stayed with me and I could tell he wondered why Rocky forged ahead without checking on us, but neither of us said anything.

Finally, I emerged from the trees at an abrupt drop-off. Thirty feet below, a river gushed through a narrow gorge, then widened, tumbling over rocks and around boulders, making its way to the lake. Rocky waited near a log that had fallen over the gorge and lodged between stone ledges, forming a bridge that spanned the twenty-foot gap.

"Is this the only place to cross?" I asked. The log seemed firmly planted but was wet with the rain.

He nodded and held out his hand for me.

"Oh, thanks, but—" I held up my hands "—I need to balance." With my arms spread out to either side like an airplane, I shuffled across.

As soon as I stepped foot on the other side, Rocky was right behind me. I swung around, my eyes wide.

"Good," he said and passed me by, continuing on at the previous pace.

Good?

Dalton came along side me. "What'd he say?"

I shrugged. "Good."

"Good?" He shook his head. "This guy's something else."

I grinned. "Maybe he's the Kushtaka."

"The what?"

"It's a Tlingit legend. Kushtaka is a half-human, half-otter shapeshifter, a deceptive spirit that lures unwary adventurers to their doom, kind of like the sirens of Homer's Odyssey. He melds with the fog and snatches souls from the wilderness."

"I buy that."

I smirked.

On this side of the gorge, the trees gave way to meadow with rocky patches covered in mosses and lichens of varied greens and textures. Red bunchberries stood out from their broad-leaved plants. This was terrain in which we could more easily keep Rocky in sight. The fog had lifted some as well and the rain had stopped.

Not far, we found him crouched in the grass, pointing to something on the ground.

"Bear," he said and I realized it was scat he was pointing at. Next to it, in the wet soil, a platter-sized footprint remained. "Not long ago. Maybe an hour."

Dalton and I scanned the hillside.

Rocky laughed. Actually, more like a sarcastic huff. "You make so much noise, any respectable animal is already miles from here." He stood back up, adjusted his pack on his shoulders, and continued on.

Dalton let him get several yards away before leaning in to whisper to me. "Which is it? Is he trying to impress us or insult us?"

"I'm not sure *he* knows."

Dalton crouched down and held his hand to the print. The bear's track was nearly twice the size of his hand with his fingers spread wide.

A draft of cool air whispered over the hilltop. "Let's keep moving," he said.

I agreed.

Over the next rise, we came to a halt. Rocky was up ahead. He'd dropped his pack and had the crossbow in hand, stalking something in the bushes. *Whoosh*—a flock of birds took flight. Ptarmigan. Rocky let an arrow fly and one dropped with a thump. He had a second arrow loaded and drawn so fast, the birds were still in range. He fired and a second bird fell from the sky.

"Holy crap," I said to Dalton.

"Holy crap is right. I've never seen anyone shoot like that."

"When Townsend said he was the best, I guess he meant it."

"The man's got skills," he said, genuinely impressed.

Rocky pulled the arrows from the birds, wiped them off in the wet grass, and carefully placed them back in the quiver. He held one of the birds by the neck, ripped it open at the wound site, peeling back its skin, shoved his thumbs inside, tore the breast meat out and tossed what was left on the ground. He did the same with the second bird, tucked the meat in a plastic sack, then hefted his pack once again and set off. Without one word to us.

"Hey Rocky," I shouted after him. "That was pretty amazing. How'd you learn to shoot like that?"

He came to a halt, slowly turned around, stood tall with a smug pride. "I could show you."

"Would you?" *Whatever, dude*.

He set his pack down and held the crossbow out for me.

I dropped my pack and approached him, but as I took hold of the bow, he kept a firm grasp on it and eased beside me. "Here, like this," he said, placing his hand over mine, making sure I held it properly.

"I get it," I said.

The thing had two grips on the bottom like an assault rifle. I positioned the butt against my shoulder, my right finger on the trigger and looked through the scope.

"It's just like shooting a gun. Just as accurate too. I keep an arrow loaded all the time."

"May I?" I said, gesturing toward a rotting, moss-covered stump about thirty yards away.

He hesitated. It might damage an arrow. Then he smiled. "Sure. For you."

I raised the weapon, both hands on the grips, bringing the sights in on the stump. I eased back the trigger and twang, the arrow released with the force of a bullet. A split second later, smack, it lodged in the soft stump.

"Wow, that is accurate," I said, genuinely impressed. "Dalton, you should give it a try."

"Well, it's not a toy," Rocky said, snatching it back from me. He stomped away, pulled the arrow from the stump, then continued on without looking back.

I shot Dalton a look. *What'd I do?*

Dalton shrugged. This guy was an enigma.

Another five hundred yards, we reached the top of a rise where he'd set up the spike camp. The area, about fifteen by twenty feet, was surrounded by an electric fence, a necessity in bear country. The fencing consisted of four wires, each about twelve or so inches apart, stretched between wooden posts, the top wire at eye level.

I dropped my pack and breathed hard to catch my breath.

"Don't tell me that little stroll got you winded," Rocky said, his eyes challenging me. "Maybe I've misjudged you. The bear I was planning to—"

"I'm fine," I said. I pointed to the fence. "That's quite the corral. Is that really necessary?"

"If you want to sleep."

The entry gate was simply the spot where each of the four strands of electric wire had a plastic handle to grab ahold and unhook from where it connected. He unhooked each, motioned for us to enter, then followed us through and set down all his gear. Without a word, he turned right around and headed down the hillside toward a copse of alders in the valley, leaving the gate open.

This lack of communication thing was annoying. "Where's he going?"

Dalton shrugged with a look of resignation. It was what it was. We were here, with this guy, for a hunt. We'd smile, act our part, then go home.

Moments later Rocky appeared pulling a wagon with a plastic storage box mounted on top. *Smart.* The electric fence was probably not visible from the air, if there was even air patrol of the park here. I'd have to check on that. But hiding some gear and not having to carry it in every time made it awfully convenient.

He wheeled the cart into camp, then snapped the electric lines back into place to reconnect. "Can't be too cautious in bear country," he said with an actual grin. He flipped open the lid, reached in, and pulled out a box. "This here's the battery. I'll get that hooked up right away, then we'll get a fire going and grill up your dinner. That sound good?"

I gave him a smile. *Sure, now he's all chatty.*

Dalton pointed at the battery. "Do you need a hand with that?"

Rocky gave no response, as if Dalton wasn't there at all. His eyes on me, he said, "Can you pitch a tent?"

"Of course," I said. I think I liked him better as the sulking, quiet type.

Dalton and I got to work setting up camp. There were only two tents, so that meant Dalton and I would be together. In the same tent. *Don't think about it.* Lying next to each other— *don't think about it!*

We stashed the guns and ammo in the plastic storage box to keep them dry and the rain had let up in time for us to get a fire going, though fresh ptarmigan wasn't something I thought I could stomach.

Rocky skewered the ptarmigan breasts and propped them over the fire. Then he stood a flimsy tripod over that, hung from it a pot he'd pulled from the storage box, filled it with water and a packet of soup from his bag.

We sat in the wet grass around the fire on our rain jackets, eating the warm soup from coffee mugs in silence as the sky grew darker and the meat slowly browned.

The plane looked tiny, resting on the placid lake. The shoreline where we'd come ashore was hidden from this view, far below us, but why would that be a problem? Why was Rocky concerned about the plane being out of sight? Bears wouldn't bother it, would they?

The fog had completely cleared and I could make out part of the route we'd taken up the hillside. A line of trees marked the gorge we'd crossed, now a dark slit amid the lush green. The rest of the hillside, yellow and green, muted into gray.

If it weren't for Rocky, I'd be content to be here, camping in the great outdoors, even though rainclouds lingered on the horizon, hiding any hint of the sunset.

When I finished the last of my soup, Rocky rinsed all the mugs in a small plastic tub, then walked several yards outside the fence to dump the rinse water. When he returned, he tucked everything away in the plastic storage box, then plopped back down by the fire, turning the meat. "We have enough daylight for one hunt a day. We'll set out at first light," he said. His eyes fell on me. "Are you ready?"

My throat started to constrict. "We already flipped a coin. My brother gets to go first."

He shook his head, his gaze locked on me like a tiger's. "I made a plan and you'll follow it."

An awkward moment passed before Dalton shrugged. "Fine with me."

"What the hell was that?" I whispered in Dalton's ear as we lay in the tent.

He shifted to whisper in mine. "I don't know. He's odd, that's for sure. But we have to play this out. Remember what you told Joe."

"I know," I said and pulled away from him. *What am I going to do?*

He moved closer. His breath hot on my neck, he said, "I'll be right there with you."

"He could be right outside the tent, listening to us," I whispered.

Dalton pressed his lips right to my ear. "I know. That's why I'm so close."

His warm body next to mine, snuggled up like a spoon, made me shiver.

"Are you cold?" he asked and inched closer to me.

"No. Yes. I mean, yes I'm cold." *Dammit.*

He put his arm over me and snugged me closer, all warm and strong and...*too close.*

I stiffened and tried to control my breathing. This thing with Dalton was getting too—

"Are you all right?"

"Yes, yes." *No! Get your head on straight, McVie.* I drew in a long breath. Maybe Dalton had a real thing for me. Maybe not. But he was a professional. He wasn't going to cross the line. Ever. He and I both knew what that would mean. The end of our careers. Yep, he was off-limits. End of story.

So why did I want so badly to roll over and—

"I know it's your first time. But we talked about this. It's part of the job."

"Huh? Yeah, I know." *Shut up about the hunting already.*

"And I've got your back. Remember? Partner?"

I nodded. *Partner.* That's what we were. Partners.

"Just get some sleep," he whispered and smoothed my hair across my ear.

Sleep? Are you kidding? With your body pressed against me? Poaching I could handle. But hiding my feelings for Dalton, well, that was another story.

CHAPTER 7

"Gear up," Rocky said after I'd scarfed down an energy bar and half a mug of coffee. He tossed me a bag of trail mix. "We've got a hike to get there."

"I'm ready," I said, stuffing the bag in my pocket.

A clear sky promised a warm, sunny day even though I could see my breath as I got my things ready to go. The sun was already bathing the landscape in pastel orange and there was no rain. The air was crisp and puffs of vapor rose from the surface of the lake. A dusting of snow had fallen on the mountain tops in the night and the highest peaks stood out like white beacons on the horizon.

Dalton handed me my rifle and slung his over his shoulder. We both had daypacks with water, snacks, and emergency gear.

Rocky had repacked his own gear and now carried a backpack, I assume with the tools to skin a bear, a knapsack, his rifle and crossbow, and now, a sidearm on his belt. He looked at me, said "Keep up," and set out.

We trekked over the hill, down into a ravine choked with knee-high brush bearing yellow leaves covered in tiny, shimmering beads of dew that soaked our pants and socks. The smell of wet moss—that distinct scent of autumn—was in the air. After we climbed another rise, we finally stopped for a break. Rocky gave us about forty-five seconds to gulp from our water bottles before pushing on again.

I thought of myself as being in pretty good shape, but this man was inhuman. With all the gear he carried, he didn't break a sweat.

Finally, he slowed as we approached an open valley, wide and dotted with patches of alder. He moved to a moss-covered boulder that stood to my waist and dropped his backpack beside it. "Stay here, armed and alert," he said and disappeared down the slope.

"What the hell?" I said to Dalton once Rocky was out of earshot.

"The guy thinks he's Rambo." Dalton crossed his arms and shook his head. "He's probably going to crawl into a bear den and wrestle him into submission."

"Rambo is right. Damn, he's fit. He moves like a machine."

"Ex-military maybe? Did you notice how he blouses his pants? And the way he wears his cap?" He smirked. "I bet he was a Ranger wash-out."

"Why is that?"

"Well, he wouldn't have made it as a SEAL."

"Right," I said, shaking my head. "Men."

Dalton shifted his stance, standing a little taller. "Hey, it's not that. SEALs have a code. You're part of a team, something greater." His eyes scanned the area where Rocky had gone. "That guy's a lone wolf."

I stared at Dalton. Wasn't that what Mr. Martin had said about me? A lone wolf? I was a problem because I go my own way, make my own decisions? Well, not this time. I was going to do my job, just like I was supposed to. Rocky was tracking the bear. Like Dalton said, he'd find it. He'd do anything it takes. There was big money at stake. And when he came back, I'd have to cross a line I never thought I would.

My throat thickened and my hands started to shake.

Dalton was watching me. He didn't say anything. He didn't have to.

I held the rifle in my hands, ran my finger along the trigger. My dad's voice came to my mind. *Sometimes we have to do things we don't like.* In the vision that came with it, I was sitting in front of a plate of broccoli. I smiled at the memory.

"What are you thinking about?" Dalton asked.

"It's funny, the things that pop into your head. My dad, he..." My hand went to the bracelet my dad had given me.

"Poppy, I know you believe your dad was killed by poachers and we're here—"

"I don't believe. I know."

He held up his hands. "I understand. I'm not saying he wasn't. My point is, being here, well, how are you doing?"

The weird thing was, I hadn't thought of my father again until now, what with my job on the line and the fiasco on the plane. But now all those feelings rushed in. "You don't know the whole story. That file, it paints a picture of my dad that isn't accurate. Like he just happened to be in the wrong place at the wrong time. It's not true. My dad had a purpose, a reason. He was passionate about what he did. Maybe he didn't know the extent of the danger he was in, but that doesn't make him an idiot."

Dalton nodded in understanding.

"An idealist, surely, but—" I sucked in my breath. My gaze locked on Dalton.

He stared back at me, his eyes filled with compassion.

I turned away. *Dammit.* "I'm not my dad."

"Okay," Dalton said. A whisper.

I spun back to face him. "It's not the same anyway."

"I know."

I can't shoot a bear.

Dalton nodded, acceptance in his expression as though he'd read my mind.

My gaze shifted to the horizon, away from this conversation, these thoughts. "Where is that guy, anyway?"

"God knows," Dalton said with a shake of his head.

About twenty awkward minutes or so passed, me pacing, Dalton examining his cuticles, before we spotted Rocky coming over the hill.

Once he got within earshot, he said, "No sign of him in that direction. But I'm going to find him for you, darlin'. You'll see. I'm going to check to the west. You just sit tight. Be ready."

"Okay," I said.

As soon as he was gone again, I turned to Dalton. "Darlin'?"

Dalton stared after him, a look of concern on his face.

"Dalton?"

"Huh?" He turned. "Yeah?"

"Darlin'?"

He just shrugged and shook his head. As soon as Rocky was out of sight again, Dalton said, "Check it out," pointing to a spot along the ridge.

"What is it?" I asked.

"I'll be right back."

"Great," I said as he moseyed away, leaving me alone with my thoughts.

As Dalton wandered away, I followed his backside, that nice, tight—*knock it off!* I spun around and looked out over the landscape in the other direction, took a deep breath, then slowly turned back toward Dalton.

About two hundred yards away he'd come to a halt. He gave me a wave with a nod. Whatever that meant. Then he seemed to be picking leaves from some bushes. No, he was picking berries.

About ten minutes later, he came back with a handful of blueberries.

"There's a whole patch of them over there," he said with a boyish grin as he took my hand in his and filled it with plump berries.

At his touch, I felt my cheeks turn pink. *Dammit!*

I tossed a few of the berries into my mouth and squished them against my tongue, enjoying the sweet and tangy taste. "Thanks," I managed, facing the other way so he couldn't see my cheeks. How embarrassing. You'd think I was ten and he was my first crush.

"I don't know where Rocky went, but any self-respecting bear in the area will be by to hit that patch of berries," Dalton said. "The branches are drooping with them."

I could only nod. That grin had left me tongue-tied.

Another four hours passed as Dalton and I leaned against the boulder, talking about nothing, my nerves on a razor's edge, before Rocky appeared again. As he approached, he didn't have the same vigor in his stride.

"I know there's a trophy bear in these parts. I've seen him. I've tracked him. I ain't lyin'." He paced, wringing his hands. "I'll find him for sure tomorrow."

Relief flooded over me, but I did my best to look disappointed.

"I won't let you down. I swear it. I'm gonna get you your bear, ya hear me?"

I managed a reassuring nod. "It's all right. We've got several more days, right?"

"Yeah, yeah. But I'll find him tomorrow. You wait and see. Tomorrow."

He was so apologetic, I almost felt bad. Almost.

Rocky marched back to camp without another word. Once inside the fence, he dropped his pack and weapons in a pile, flipped open the lid of the box, and stomped back and forth, hanging his head as he built a fire.

He hung the pot over the flames and attacked the soup packaging, ripping it open with his knife, then shook the contents into the pot, crumpled the bag and tossed it to the ground.

Dalton and I watched in silence, avoiding any interaction, fearing it might irritate him even more.

Once the soup was ready, he dished it out, handing us the mugs without eye contact.

Pushing his issues from my mind, I wrapped my hands around the mug of soup, enjoying the warmth, and inhaled the Asian-spiced scent of the broth. When I drank it down, nothing had ever tasted as good. Something about being out all day in the fresh air, the physical exertion, that makes anything with nourishment and extra salt taste heavenly.

While we ate, Rocky poured over a map and journal, his notes, I assumed, from his scouting expeditions to find bears. He probably kept accounts of every sighting, every direction, time of day, trying to understand the habits of any particular bear. Like Dalton had said, there was big money on the table.

After Rocky had rinsed our dishes and packed up camp for the night, he headed for his tent. He unzipped the fly, and without turning to face me, he said, "Tomorrow. I'll prove myself to you tomorrow," and crawled in.

The next morning, we set out again for the same boulder. With the same strategy, Rocky left us alone to track the bear.

Dalton whispered to me. "I hope he brings in a bear today. I'm not sure what he'll do if he doesn't."

"I was thinking the same thing," I said, but if I was honest, I'd rather have had to deal with a disgruntled Rocky than have to kill a bear. I was content to lean against that rock next to Dalton, the sun on my face, and let the day slip away in uneventful bliss. But deep down, I knew it wouldn't. I was going to have to face it. There was no crawling back out of the rabbit hole.

I leaned my head back and closed my eyes. *What the holy hell am I going to do?*

About an hour later, Rocky appeared, coming up over the bluff, heading for us at a pretty good clip, shouting and gesturing for me to raise my weapon.

Dalton turned toward me. "It's time. You ready, Poppy?"

My heart thrummed in my chest. I nodded and placed my rifle on the boulder, using it to steady myself.

"Get ready," Rocky said as he approached.

No! No, no, no. "I was born ready." My nerves buzzed up and down my arms.

He looked at me from under his cap. "I mean be alert. Ready. He's coming." He said it in a creepy voice like we were in a Stephen King film. Man, these guys were all about the drama, the thrill.

From his knapsack he pulled out some kind of remote control box that had a fancy joystick and a video monitor.

A surge of anger rushed through me. This asshole had a drone.

"Dude," Dalton said with a full-fledged, dumbass-grin. "That is kick ass."

"Be ready," Rocky warned, fiddling with the joystick.

As soon as I heard the whir of the drone, the bear emerged on the hill across from us, about four hundred yards away, running full speed toward me, all muscle, fur and teeth. He could cover the distance between us in twenty seconds. My heart went into overdrive, sending adrenaline coursing through my veins. I swear I could hear my heartbeat vibrating against my eardrums. I gripped the rifle handle and told myself to breathe.

Rocky worked the drone, steering it to dive-bomb the

bear. The bear spun on it and reared up, swiping at it with his monster-sized paw. Rocky managed to work the drone just out of the bear's reach, making him swat at it again and again, getting him frustrated and angry. All for the excitement, so a poacher could shoot a charging bear.

"Ready?" Rocky said.

I managed to nod, my finger on the trigger, shaking.

The drone swooped downward and the bear started to chase it, but then turned. The drone zoomed upward, then swooped back downward toward the bear, making him run again. The bear took three strides, then dropped to the ground, spun around again, and roared. The bear's rage rumbled down my spine.

"C'mon, you bastard," Rocky said, working the controller. I wanted to yank it from his hands and slam it into his face.

The drone dipped and buzzed, spun around the bear's head like a giant bee, until it pushed him into a run again.

"You got him now," Dalton said with a whoop.

"He's a trophy, girl," Rocky grunted. "Get ready. All nine hundred pounds of him are headed this way."

The drone zoomed from left to right, keeping the bear on a path straight for me. The poor thing didn't have a chance. What the hell kind of hunt was this? How could anyone think this was fun?

"Get him in your sights," Rocky growled.

I leaned over the gun and looked through the scope, my heart pounding. The bear was moving closer, and fast.

"Shoot!" Rocky pushed. "Hundred fifty yards, take him."

All fur and muscle, bearing down on me. Brown eyes, enraged and angry. I aimed, blinked, holding my breath. I pulled to the side and above his head, and fired.

The sound of the rifle ricocheted off the hills, echoing in the distance.

The bear skidded to a stop fifty yards away.

Rocky dropped his hands to his sides. "You missed? Really?"

The bear huffed and snapped his jaws, swinging his head from side to side, white froth dripping from his mouth.

I tried to reload, but my hands were shaking like crazy.

The bear lowered his head and charged. Dalton stood up to his full height, raised his arms, and shouted at the bear. About twenty feet from us, the bear threw his weight and turned away.

I let out my breath. It was a bluff. *Run, bear, run! Run away!*

Kaboom! Boom, boom, boom! Rocky was beside me, his sidearm raised, unloading the clip into the bear. The big bruin staggered sideways and collapsed on the ground with a grunt.

I was shaking so hard I couldn't get words out.

Dalton was there. "What the hell, dude? He turned. You could have brought him back around again."

Rocky holstered his gun, swung around and locked on me. "You choked." He shook his head, disappointed, then something shifted in him. His demeanor changed, the way he stood. His eyes turned glassy and seemed to pass right through me.

Dalton got in his face. "Hey, give her a break, man."

Rocky took a step closer to me, not just ignoring Dalton, but passing him by as though he didn't exist. "It's too bad," he said, his voice like gravel. "I hoped you'd be different than all the rest."

Dalton stepped between us. "Hey, I'm talking to you. What the hell is your problem?"

Rocky lifted his eyes to meet mine. They narrowed and shifted into focus. "What a disappointment." He curled up his lip in disgust. His eyes traveled down my body, then slowly back up and I felt ripped bare. "You don't even realize it," he growled as he took a strand of my hair in his hand and twirled it through his fingers. "If it wasn't for me, you'd be dead." His eyes darkened. "Out here, it's kill or be killed."

CHAPTER 8

Dalton wedged himself between me and Rocky. "Dude, back the hell off already!"

Rocky blinked his eyes and blinked again, then hung his head, the shy outcast returning.

While Dalton and I exchanged uncomfortable glances, Rocky rummaged through his pack for tools to skin the bear. "The scent of blood will bring 'em running," he said to Dalton, shoving his rifle at him. "Cover me. I'll be quick about it."

He warily approached the bear, then kicked it with his boot to make sure it was dead. I turned away but couldn't escape the sounds as he sawed at the skin and ripped open the hide.

"It's all right, Sis. You'll get one next time," Dalton said, his eyes scanning the hills. "You got buck fever, that's what you done. Happens to lots of people." He grinned. "Except me of course."

One thing about Dalton: he could stay in character.

He gave me a reassuring wink. "I bet Rocky here can keep a secret," he went on. "We don't have to tell nobody you choked."

"I didn't choke," I said. "I just—I just missed. Okay."

Rocky's hands were covered in blood. He had the two front paws sawed off of the bear and was working on a foot.

I glanced at Dalton, my head still spinning from Rocky's bizarre behavior. I managed to get my thoughts in order. We were poachers. Unethical, greedy poachers. "I guess that'll still make a nice rug."

"Now you're talking," Dalton said with a nod.

Rocky paused, but didn't look up at me. "Too late," he muttered and went back at it.

"Well, what, that's it then?" I said. "Will I get another shot? Will you find another bear?" *God, please say no.*

"Dunno," Rocky said, dropping the severed leg and lifting the last one to remove the paw.

"What are you doing there, anyway?" I asked even though I knew. Bears paws were worth a fortune on the black market. In Korea, they have been considered an exotic delicacy since the ancient dynasties, reserved only for the elite. A bowl of bear paw soup can sell for as much as one thousand dollars.

"Taking my pay," he said. He plunged his knife into the bear's gut, made a slice, then reached into the entrails and pulled out the gall bladder. He didn't have to fish around. He knew exactly how to get to it. He'd done this many times before.

A gall bladder was worth more than the paws on the black market. Some believe the bile can cure all kinds of ailments, though modern science proves otherwise.

"Open my pack and get some water to rinse my hands," he said to me. There was no please.

I doused his hands, trying not to look at the gall bladder. He stuffed it into a Ziploc bag, along with the paws, hefted his backpack, and said, "Let's go."

"That's it?" I asked. "What about the carcass?" The bear lay there, his blood soaking the ground, his vacant eyes staring at nothing.

He jerked his head toward the forest. "Something'll eat it," he said, turned his back to me and walked away.

Once we arrived back in camp, Rocky got a fire going and hung a pot of water to boil for coffee. The guide once again.

A cold, drizzly rain fell like mist. I sat down on the tarp next to the fire, holding my hands to the flame, trying to get rid of the chill and at the same time keep them from shaking.

Rocky dumped a spoonful of coffee grounds into the pot, then slung his rifle over his shoulder. "I'll be back to get dinner going. Gotta check in."

"What? You're leaving us here?" I said, getting to my feet.

"You'll be fine. The fence is on." He looked at me from under his cap. "I just forgot the satellite phone in the plane is all."

Something about his tone was off. He was trying too hard to be cordial. "Oh, yeah, okay," I said with a smile. "We'll be here."

Dalton and I watched him in silence as he trudged down the hill, then disappeared on the other side, then reappeared as he crossed the river on the log bridge.

"I've got a bad feeling about this," I whispered to Dalton, even though Rocky was more than five hundred yards away by now. "He didn't leave the phone in the plane. I'm sure he's had it with him all along. Shit, what if we're blown?"

Dalton, calm as can be, said, "We stay the course."

"And what the hell was that all about after he shot the bear? This guy's a serious head case."

Dalton nodded in agreement, concern in his eyes.

"I know this is an important case, but I don't think I can spend another day out here with him. He's giving me the creeps."

"I don't like him either. That's why I'm not going to leave your side." He flashed me a smile and his gaze dropped to my chest, ever so briefly. "So try to enjoy it." He turned away abruptly, as though catching himself. His eyes swept over the landscape. "It's gorgeous out here."

I took the opportunity to enjoy his backside, how his hiking pants fit snugly over the nice curve of his ass. As he turned back, my eyes snapped to the lake. "It is beautiful, but Rocky's ruined it all. Do you think he's really calling Townsend and he just didn't want us to hear the conversation?"

I could see Dalton's mind turning over the possibility. "Maybe."

"We're blown. That's what it is. I blew it."

Dalton looked me in the eyes, strong and steady. "We stay the course." He waited for me to nod confirmation. "There's nothing to indicate our cover is blown. People choke and miss all the time."

I nodded. "You're right. He's just so...weird."

"Well, there's that. But Poppy—" he gave his full attention to our conversation "—we're going to stay the course. You with me?"

I inhaled and blew out my breath with a sigh. "Yeah. I'm with you."

The campfire popped and crackled. Dalton used a stick to give it a stir and stuffed another log under the hanging pot. He stood up and ran his fingers through his hair, all curly from the misty rain.

I chewed on my fingernail. Yep, I needed to figure out what to do. Being with Dalton like this, damn, it was going to get me in trouble. But then again, maybe it wouldn't matter. I was probably going to be fired anyway. This op was going nowhere, and as soon as I got back, I had to face an investigation. There was nothing I could do now but power through this and keep my cover—

"Shit, Dalton." I threw my hands up. "He's suspicious. That's what it is. He's going to tell Townsend. I should have—"

"We don't know that." He shook his head as though something wasn't adding up. "Listen. If he suspected us, why would he still take the paws and gall bladder? Right in front of us?"

"I don't know. Maybe he's cocky and thinks the evidence to corroborate our story is being devoured by ravens and wolves right now."

Dalton rested his hands on his hips and stared in the direction Rocky had gone. "But being caught with the bear parts would be enough for a conviction. He'd know that. So why's he going to the plane? To stash the goods? And why did he anchor the plane out where he could see it instead of leaving it on shore? What's he worried about?"

"Good question." I scanned the landscape around us. All hills and forest. No sign of humans save for the aroma of our fresh coffee in the air. "We are literally in the middle of nowhere. No one is going to come along and steal the plane. They'd have to arrive by another plane to do it."

Dalton spun around. "The radio."

"You think he's using the radio on the plane? To call another plane? Maybe to pick up the bear parts?" I looked out at the plane floating on the lake. Rocky should be almost to it by now, but it was getting too dark to see anything on the surface of the lake.

"I don't know," Dalton said, hands on his hips again, his eyes traveling to the storage box. "It doesn't really make sense." He turned to face me. "Maybe he's planning to make a call on the sat phone, but not to Townsend." He shrugged. "Or maybe he really forgot the phone. Maybe it's legit."

"I don't believe anything's legit with that guy." All I could think about was the bear, charging toward me, then turning, scared, and him firing away. I gnashed my teeth together. "Kill or be killed. What an ass. That bear turned away. It was running away."

"He had it pretty aggravated." Dalton's attention was on me now. "We don't know what it would have done."

"Don't tell me you're defending him. There wasn't an

imminent threat. It was clearly a bluff. The bear had turned."

"I know," he said, holding his hands up in mock surrender. "I'm just saying that it was a dangerous situation, like we talked about. If it would have turned back again, and headed toward you, we would've had only seconds. If that happened, I would've—"

"But it didn't." I pressed my lips together, trying not to get emotional. "That bear had already backed down. To kill it like he did was…"

Dalton smiled at me, his eyes lingering on mine.

I frowned. "What?"

"You."

His expression changed, unexpected. He wasn't arguing with me or trying to convince me. He was—I don't know. "Me what?"

He stepped toward me. The way his eyes held mine made my pulse jump. "That bear was twenty feet away, in a rage, and you still believed, right up 'til the last second that it was a bluff charge. You truly are an optimist."

"Optimist. Ha!" I turned from his gaze. "That's what gets me in trouble."

"I wish I could be more like you."

"Don't mock me." I didn't need another lecture right now.

"Never," he said, putting his hands on my shoulders and gently pulling me toward him. "Look at me."

Something in his tone, a softness, made me give in. I turned toward him and raised my eyes to meet his.

"Don't ever lose that. You don't see the predator, like everyone else does, as a mindless killer." He took my hand and held it between his warm hands. "You see the beautiful being within."

"You think I'm naive." I pulled my hand away. "Don't talk to me like I'm a child."

"No," he said, shaking his head and taking my hand again.

This time, the feel of his hands on mine, the look in his eyes, stirred a fire inside me, one I ached to give in to. "Not at all. I'm saying I'm trying, trying not to always see the bad, the dark, the evil in everything. I wish I could see the good, the beauty in things, like you do. But when you've seen what I've seen, you think only in terms of survival, how you'll live to breathe another day." He smiled, a soft, resigned smile. "Then someone like you comes along." His eyes were clear, honest. "And you make me feel like life's worth living again."

"Well, I..." My cheeks flushed pink. *Damn cheeks!*

"I mean it, Poppy. Honest. It's what I...it's what I love about you."

My insides tingled. *Did he just say what I think he said?* His eyes on me felt so comfortable, so right.

The fire sparked. The pop made me pull back with a jerk, but Dalton held onto my hand, gentle yet strong. A warm electricity radiated from his hand to mine. He wasn't letting go.

A tiny dimple creased his cheek, enhanced by the light from the fire, as he smiled at me, his eyes locked with mine. He leaned toward me. A little closer. My heart raced and my hand felt tingly.

"Dalton, I don't think—"

"We have time."

Standing so close to me, I could feel his desire, like sparks shooting through the air between us. But he was off-limits. But god, he would be so worth it. But no, he was off-limits.

"We need to be careful. This op, my job—"

"Yeah and I could get fired just for what I'm thinking right now," he said with a mischievous grin that made my insides flush with heat, firing up places that shouldn't be fired up.

He stepped closer to me, so close I could feel his breath on my face. Our clothes were the only thing between us, the only barrier. Wow, it was hot out here. Like the heat stirred up from a tropical hurricane. And I was in the center of it, in the eye of the storm.

He cupped my cheek in his hand and his gaze lingered on my lips as his finger traced my jaw. I couldn't breathe. His eyes made their way back to mine as the tip of his finger lightly brushed my lips.

Then he paused. Was he having second thoughts? Pulling back? The corner of his mouth was still turned up into that irresistible grin. Was he amused? Already feeling regret?

Shut up, brain!

He'd dropped his gaze back to my lips and his breath came in short puffs.

I couldn't take the anticipation anymore. I surrendered to it. I reached around his neck, pulled us closer, and kissed him. He responded to me with the same passion, slipping his hands from my hips to my lower back, pulling me tight against him. His lips, his warm tongue, the feel of his stubble, rough on my face, sent shivers of desire up and down my spine. I pushed my fingers through the curls at the back of his neck, holding on.

I couldn't get enough, couldn't get close enough. I wanted him. Passion rippled through me like wildfire. I tugged at his shirt.

"Ah, well, isn't this interesting." A voice behind us.

I flung myself away from Dalton, my chest heaving.

Rocky stood there, a strange grin on his face, his sidearm in his hand, pointed at Dalton.

"Well, well, well." He moved toward us.

Shit! Our situation, the op—Dalton's supposed to be my brother. *We're blown! Oh shit! Oh shit!* I tried to move but my knees turned to rubber, like I was fighting quicksand. How did he get inside the wires without us noticing?

Dalton side-stepped away, putting space between us—textbook procedure for one assailant. At least he had his wits about him.

Rocky's eyes were locked on me, but he managed to keep the weapon trained on Dalton. "I admit, I wasn't expecting that." His eyes narrowed. He was thinking, considering some idea. The firelight flickered on his face, making him seem even more menacing. "Can't blame you," he said to Dalton. "She is one hot little tomcat. I plan to have a little fun with her myself." He turned his head toward Dalton and raised the gun to aim. "But you'd be in the way."

No! I lunged forward and kicked the boiling pot into the air. Hot coffee splashed in his face. He reared back, yelping, stumbled and fell. As he hit the ground, flat on his back, he fired blindly into the air.

"Run!" I yelled.

Chapter 9

I spun toward the gate. It was open. I ran so fast I couldn't believe my legs kept up with me. Dalton was right behind me, hollering, "Go, go, go!"

Shots fired in the air. I ducked. Adrenaline surged through my veins and spurred me on. I zigged left, heading for a copse of alders for some cover. One stride, then another, then another and I plunged into the brush, my heart hammering in my chest, branches slapping me in the face.

"Get down," Dalton was saying, right on my heels. "Get down!"

I dropped to my hands and knees, pushing through the brambles.

"Hold up," Dalton said, grabbing my ankle.

"Are you crazy?" I dug my elbows into the ground, pulling myself along.

"He's not following us."

"What?" I halted, listening.

"Damn. He's smart," Dalton said. "Just sit tight a minute."

"Sit tight?" I gasped, catching my breath. "You can't be serious."

"Shhh. Listen."

I held my breath. A wolf howled, a long mournful note. Then a yip-yip-yip, followed by another long, drawn out yowl. It was coming from the camp.

"Is that—?"

"The crazy bastard knows he's got us."

At once, I realized Dalton was right. Rocky had no reason to chase us down. He'd lose his advantage. In the camp, he had food, fire, shelter. He had all the weapons.

We had nothing.

And it was dusk already. Soon it'd be pitch dark. "Shit, Dalton. What were we thinking?" *How could I be so stupid?* "How did we let him sneak up on us like that? I thought he was half a mile away."

"Me too." He pushed back some branches, shifting to get a better view. "Me too."

"But now he knows we're agents!"

"We don't know that."

"He just caught us kissing! Seriously, Dalton? You think the brother-sister tryst is the most believable story here?"

Dalton's eyes never left Rocky, who stoked the fire, calm as can be. "It doesn't mean he thinks we're agents. Never assume."

"He pulled his weapon." I shook my head. "We're screwed." *Shit!*

Dalton turned to face me. "Maybe it was—" His eyes fixed on my forehead. "You okay?" With his hand on my chin, he turned my head to examine my face.

I wiped at a trickle of blood on my forehead. "Just a scrape from a branch."

"It sliced your skin pretty good," he said, concerned.

"I'm fine."

He frowned and turned back, his eyes trained on the camp, on making sure Rocky was still there. "Maybe it was a knee-jerk reaction. Maybe he had already planned to confront us for some reason. We don't know."

"Well, what's it matter? We screwed up. Big time. And now we're out here and he's back there. With all the guns."

"It matters because it will help us anticipate his next move."

"His next move? Seriously? You think he's already got a strategic plan?"

"I don't know." He rubbed his chin. "Depends." He turned to me again. "What'd he say exactly?"

I pushed up next to him so I could get a better view of the camp. "When? When he pulled the gun?"

"Yeah."

"I don't know. Something about me being a wild cat. Some crap about taking his turn."

"Exactly."

"Exactly what?" What did that have to do with it?

Dalton patted his pants, front and back, then sorted through his jacket pockets. "I've got a jackknife," he said. "What about you?"

I smacked him on the arm. "Earth to Dalton. Exactly what?"

"That's not what a poacher would say when he realizes you're an agent."

"Well, maybe…" The memory rattled around in my brain. The look on Rocky's face wasn't surprise. It was…amusement? "I guess you're right. What do you think it means?"

"Don't know for sure. I'm just trying to assess the situation. Did he say anything to you back at the lodge? Anything at all that might make sense of this?"

"Not really. No. He probably said a total of three words to me before we got into the plane with him. He was always with Townsend, standing behind him and—oh crap."

"What?"

"Do you think he's angry that I complained about having to hunt with him? So angry he'd shoot at me?"

Dalton cocked his head to the side, considering this. "You did a pretty good job of dismissing him."

"But to shoot at me for it?"

"I don't know. You challenged his manhood, his skills as a hunter. People have killed for much less."

I shook my head. "But that doesn't make sense either. He had the gun pointed at you."

Dalton nodded, concern etched across his face. "Yeah. I know." He puzzled a moment, then gestured toward my pockets. "What do you have on you?"

I unzipped my coat pockets, one at a time and produced a baggie of trail mix with about one handful left, a tube of lip balm, and some tissues. That was it. Our daypacks, with all our emergency survival gear, were back at the camp, inside our tent. I patted my coat for any forgotten pockets and my hand fell on the necklace around my neck and the tiny compass pendant that hung there. *Oh Chris, I really screwed up this time.*

A melodic whistle came our way from the camp. A lazy, ho-hum kind of tune, as though Rocky purposefully wanted us to know how cozy he was back in camp.

"He's a nut job. That's why this doesn't make sense." I shivered, suddenly realizing how cold I was. My pants from my knees down were soaking wet. I pulled my jacket tight around me and snugged the collar up over my face. The pungent scent of woodsmoke filled my nose and made me feel even colder.

Dalton moved closer to me and I thought he was going to put his arms around me, but then he didn't. "We need to stay warm. As soon as it's good and dark, we'll move to a new location. Not far. Where I can keep an eye on him."

"What do you mean, not far? I vote for getting the hell out of here."

"And go where?" Dalton said. "There's nothing for hundreds of miles in any direction. Glacier-covered mountains to the south and west, open ocean to the east, and marshy bog to the north. The odds are pretty good we'd die out there."

"What about the plane? Don't you know how to fly it? You were a SEAL. Doesn't that stand for sea, air, land? Air as in fly?"

"They taught us how to jump out of an airplane, not how to fly it." He ran his fingers through his hair, his tell. He was frustrated, trying to sort this out.

"Don't ever play poker," I said.

"What?" He pulled away to look at me. "Poker? What are you—"

"Nothing. Sorry." I pulled the jacket tighter.

"Are you cold?" he asked. "You're cold." He put his arm around me, hesitated as if waiting for me to object, then snuggled me tight to him. "We need to keep warm," he said.

"I know," I replied, wondering why it felt so awkward all of a sudden. He had just kissed me. Or rather, I'd kissed him. I was sure he'd wanted to—*oh hell, what a mess.*

"I want to know what he's up to," Dalton said. "See if I can figure out what he's planning. I bet, at least for now, he'll stay where he is. He'll protect the weapons and gear and let us get cold and tired. If he comes out, he risks one of us circling back and taking possession of the camp."

"You know, maybe being agents is an advantage. Maybe we should threaten him with jail time, tell him how much more trouble he'll be in when they send a team out looking for us. Encourage him to go in peacefully. Right now, we could promise a misdemeanor charge, which would probably get thrown out anyway."

The whistling came again, this time with long, sorrowful notes.

Dalton shook his head. "I don't know. I don't think this guy…"

"You don't think this guy what? It could work. Maybe he doesn't know the law. Maybe he'll believe us."

"I bet he knows the law better than we do. No"—he shook his head again—"if we admit we're agents, we put Joe at risk. All Rocky has to do is call Townsend."

"How do we know he won't do that anyway? Or that he hasn't already?"

Dalton frowned. "Good point." He turned to me. "Doesn't matter though. First rule of undercover work—"

"Never reveal your cover. I know," I said.

"We need to move."

"Are you sure?" I didn't want to let go of Dalton and the relative safety I'd felt for the last two minutes. "For all we know he has night-vision binoculars."

"He might. But right now, he knows where we are for sure. If we move, at least we'll have some advantage."

He was right of course. He was a SEAL. Trained by the best military in the world. If he had a plan, it would be a good one. Maybe it was time to trust. Like Mr. Martin said, *be a team player.* "Okay," I said. "You're the SEAL."

"What's that supposed to mean?"

"It means I'm being a team player. You're trained in strategic combat tactics, reconnaissance, et cetera, et cetera, right? I'm just saying, I'll follow you."

"Right," he said, pausing a moment as if he thought there was a catch, but then seemed to accept my explanation and moved to a crouch. Hunched over, he slipped through the alders, quiet as a cat. I followed, trying not to make a sound. We pushed through the back side of the copse and ran up a rise, then circled back to a spot with downed trees and a pile of brush and hunkered down behind a log where we could see Rocky's campfire.

The darkness enveloped us like a protective cloak. My hands shook. I blew on them, trying to get them warm, then shoved them in my pants pockets. My gloves lay on the grass, back in camp, next to the fire. The warm fire.

Dalton leaned against a stump and took my hand and pulled me down to sit between his legs, his arms around me. "We need to stay warm. It's important," he said. "Our worst enemy out here is hypothermia."

"Not the guy shooting at us?"

Dalton smirked. "Yeah, other than that." He snugged me tighter. "I'm serious. The rain and wind are not our friends. If we get soaking wet, we'll lose body heat twenty times faster than just in cold air."

He was right. In an instant, we'd been plunged into a serious survival situation. If Rocky didn't get us, and we weren't careful, the wilderness would. We had to think of every move in terms of life and death.

Snuggling with Dalton, though, felt a lot like heaven.

After I got situated where I could see the camp as well, I asked, "So what are you thinking?"

"He's smart. If he didn't leave camp before, he's not going to in the dark, but we should take turns on watch, just in case."

I nodded. "That's fine, but come morning, what's our plan?"

"I'm thinking."

"We're going to have to lure him out and subdue him on our own. I don't see any other option."

"But how? With what? He's got all the weapons, remember. This terrain is mostly open hills. There aren't many places to hide for an ambush and he'd never fall for it anyway."

I gritted my teeth together. "Well, what do you suggest?"

"I'm still thinking." A long moment passed, then he said, "We need to better understand the situation."

"You just said yourself, he's got the guns. We have none. He's got the food. We have none. He's got my warm, snuggly sleeping bag. And I've got—"

He pulled me closer. "I mean his mindset."

"His mindset is he doesn't want to go to prison. I say we try to make a deal."

"Maybe." Dalton wasn't convinced. "We'll see. In the morning. Maybe he'll talk."

"I'll take the first watch," I said and leaned into Dalton. Even with his arms wrapped around me, there was no way I was going to get any sleep. My mind was spinning in too many directions but mainly...*what the hell just happened?*

Denali's peak rose out of the northern horizon and seemed to join the stars. The moon shimmered across the lake and, despite the cold rain that fell earlier, the air had a hint of warmth and was filled with the scents of autumn. This could have been a perfect night.

If it weren't for that crazy man with the guns.

CHAPTER 10

The sun rises slowly in the northern latitudes, but today it felt like an interminable wait before it was high enough in the sky to confirm Rocky was sitting on his camp chair, not just a silhouette figure we'd assumed was him. He lounged, drinking a cup of coffee as though it was just another day camping in the great Alaskan wilderness.

Nothing had changed all night. But at least, after we'd moved, we were farther away and on higher ground if he would have left the camp and come after us. Dalton was adamant that we move back into the stand of alder before sunrise. He said being there would make us look less skilled, like we'd stayed there all night with no vantage point, and added that it was a better place to hide my location if I was going to try to talk to Rocky.

I couldn't argue with that logic. We didn't have a lot of choices.

I rubbed my hands together, trying to get warm. I drew in a deep breath and my nose filled with the aroma of fresh coffee and frying bacon. My stomach rumbled. *Geez, buddy. Nothing like enjoying your stay.*

"Here's what I want you to do," Dalton said. "When you speak to him, no matter what, I want you to keep your head down. Stay hidden from sight. Do you understand? I'll be the eyes."

"Sure, I guess. But won't he be able to pinpoint my location by my voice?"

"Maybe. He'll know the general area you are anyway. But if you stay hidden, he'll be watching for you. That's what we want. Him looking for you, not for me."

"What? Why? What are you going to be doing?"

"Assessing the situation."

"Right." I nodded. "Wait, what? Where will you be?"

"I won't be far. Just far enough where he won't spot me while he's looking for you."

"Okay," I said. That made sense. I supposed.

"Are you all right?" Dalton asked.

"Yeah," I nodded. "Yes." Trust your partner, that's what I was doing. What was that old saying, too many chiefs? I was going to do my best.

"Give me two minutes," he said, then belly crawled away from me through the brush.

I waited. Then waited some more, listening to Rocky whistle that same damn lazy tune while I plucked some twigs from my hair.

Maybe Dalton was right. Maybe Rocky hadn't called Townsend. Maybe this wasn't about us being agents. I shook my head. Of course it was.

Enough time had passed for Dalton to get into place. It was now or never. "Rocky!" I shouted.

Nothing. Certainly he could hear me. There was no doubt. I could hear his whistling from here. Which had stopped. What was he doing?

"Rocky!" I shouted again, into the cold air.

No acknowledgment. I wanted to crawl over to Dalton to see what was going on, but I'd promised to stay hidden.

A raven called in the distance, breaking the eerie silence.

"Listen, this is crazy. Let's talk about the situation."

Nothing. I stared at the tangle of alder branches surrounding me, keeping me hidden, yet keeping me from seeing what was happening. I felt like a sitting duck. What if Rocky was coming for me right now?

This wasn't working. We were getting nowhere. *No. Trust Dalton. He's watching.*

The whistling started again, a strange tune, like a New Orleans funeral dirge. I imagined him cleaning the weapons, part by part, and reassembling them, a creepy grin on his face.

Well, what the hell, here goes. "Look. I know you can hear me. I want you to know, we're not upset. Things just got a little out of hand. There's no reason we can't forget the whole thing. What do you say?"

The whistling stopped. What was he doing now? Dalton had completely disappeared in the brush. Too far away. *Dammit.* What was going on? Something wasn't right. I could feel it.

I rose, just to get a peek, make sure Rocky was still in the camp. I took one step to the right and bang—a shot fired, then a burning sensation seared though my upper thigh. I looked down. Blood was soaking my pant leg. I dropped to the ground and the pain hit me full force, like a hot ice pick had been shoved into my leg. I tried to breathe. Then Dalton was there, hovering over me.

"I told you to stay hidden," he said, his voice urgent.

"I... you...I just..." My breath returned in a rush. "God that hurts!"

He ripped my pant leg open and took my hand. "Squeeze my hand."

Breathe. Breathe. The pain.

"Squeeze my hand."

Oh my god, he shot me.

"Squeeze my hand!"

I clenched his hand with all my strength.

"Good." He moved my hand to my thigh. "Now squeeze

here and don't let go."

I did as he said and hot fire shot down my leg. My body clenched and I was in his arms and he was running, pushing through the branches.

"It's all right, I've got you. I've got you," he kept saying.

Blurry. Everything a blur. I clamped my eyes shut. My entire being flushed in agony, radiating from my thigh. Waves of dizzying nausea hit me, then the pull of sleep. Oh to escape to the bliss of peaceful, painless sleep. Darkness on all sides.

"Stay with me," Dalton said, shaking me. "Stay with me."

I was lying on the cold ground. Dalton knelt over me, his chest bare. Why was his chest bare?

He tugged at my thigh, a tightening, and the pain shot to my head, jolting me from my grogginess. I screamed out.

"That. Hurts," I managed, my hands going to my thigh.

"Good," he said, putting his coat back on over his bare torso. "That means you're not in complete shock."

Was that relief I saw on his face? I tried to sit up and the blood drained from my head.

"No, no, no," he said. "Stay right where you are."

"But, Rocky, he shot me. He's—" I blinked my eyes, trying to focus. "We have to get out of here."

"It's all right. He hasn't left the camp."

"I didn't think he'd actually—" I looked down at the bloody mess of my thigh. Dalton had tied a tourniquet above the wound. "I should've listened to you. He tried to kill me."

"I don't think so," Dalton said.

"What?" He wasn't making any sense. "He shot me."

"I know."

I got my hands underneath me and pushed myself up.

"Easy now. You're safe right where you are. Sit back."

We were on the bank of a tiny stream that trickled down the hillside with a lazy gurgle. Pieces of Dalton's shirt lay on the ground in torn, bloody hunks.

"I think I got it cleaned good. The bullet went right through. Brushed you really. You're lucky." He ripped a clean piece of the shirt and tied it around the wound for a bandage.

"Lucky? He shot me!"

Dalton grinned. "Welcome to the club."

I looked down at the bloody bandage. "Damn that hurts."

Dalton winked. "You need to rest. And don't move that leg. I don't have any way to suture it."

He took my hand and dumped the trail mix into it. "Eat that."

"No." I protested. "It's all we've got. You need some."

"You eat it all," he said. "I'm fine." Then a pause. "You said you'd follow me. Right? I say you eat it."

I did as he told me, crunching nuts between my teeth.

He dunked the baggie into the stream and brought it to my mouth. "Take a drink."

"But is it safe?"

He shrugged. "We'll worry about giardia later. You need to drink."

I sipped the ice cold water and glanced around. "Where are we?"

"Out of sight," he said. "For now." He looked over his shoulder as he gathered the bloody rags and tossed them into the stream. "But we need to move. Too much blood scent here."

"But you just said—"

"Bears. One gets your scent, he won't look so cuddly." He rinsed his hands in the stream, then turned to me. "I want to head uphill. We'll have to see if you can make it. I might need to carry you."

"Carry me? No," I said, trying to get up. Fresh agony brought me back to my seat.

He reached down and swooped me up in his arms like I was a toddler.

"I'll take my chances with a bear," I said, half meaning it.

"You'll change your mind when he bares his teeth."

I might have been delirious, or in shock, but something was bothering Dalton more than concern about a bear. "What is it?" I said. "Something's wrong. I can tell."

"I need for you to listen to me is all. To trust me." He pulled me close to his chest and headed up the hill. "We could die out here, you know."

I nodded. I knew the trouble we were in. "I'm sorry, Dalton. I misread him. Honestly, I thought we could talk to him. I didn't think he'd really try to kill me."

Dalton grimaced. There it was again. Something he wasn't telling me.

"Just hold on to me," he said, and headed for higher ground.

"No, you tell me. What's the matter?"

He pulled me a little tighter to his chest.

"Dammit, Dalton. I promise I'll listen. I'll follow. I'll do as you say, from here on out. But don't you dare keep me in the dark. What is it?"

He slowed, looked down at me. "The distance. With that weapon. He could have killed you. Easily."

"What are you saying? That he's not a killer? He's just trying to warn us? Scare us? That's a good thing, right?"

"I'm not sure." He shook his head, pulled me back tight to his chest, and started walking again. "I'm not sure."

Chapter 11

Overhead, an unkindness of ravens circled. An odd term for birds. A group of crows is called a murder. But ravens are even more sophisticated, more intuitively clever. An unkindness seemed appropriate right now, as they circled, seemingly uncaring of our plight.

Would they let us know if Rocky was on the move? Would they side with him? If he's as good a tracker as he claimed, would he pop up and slit our throats before we even knew he was there? Perhaps the ravens would swoop in to pluck our eyes out while we were still warm.

Dalton found what he was looking for, a protected spot where we could hunker down and he could see in multiple directions. The sun had already moved to the west. It was late afternoon. I must have been out of it for longer than I thought.

He put me down on the moss, then sat, his back against a rock embankment, and gestured for me to snug up against him. "We need to stay warm," he said, opening his jacket so I could lean against his bare chest.

Yeah, you keep saying that... "But you won't be able—"

"Just do it, McVie. You're at risk of hypothermia. No arguing."

I scooted between his legs and leaned against him and he wrapped his arms and coat around us both.

The coat didn't quite cover me. "Closer," he said.

I shifted on my thigh, sending sharp spines of pain into my hip. I panted, trying to endure it.

"Easy now," he whispered.

Leaning against his chest, finally able to relax, I could feel the tension in him. He was scanning the hills, watching, waiting.

"So before, when you said he could have killed me, but he didn't, you meant that he chose to shoot me in the leg when he had a clear chest shot. You think he missed on purpose." It was a half question, half statement.

Dalton nodded. "I do."

"That's good news then. He doesn't want to kill us."

"Not sure."

"You said that but—"

"Listen," he said, carefully shifting to get a better view over my shoulder. "Let's focus on what we know for sure. That he knows he hit you. We need to use it to our advantage."

"Okay. How?" I swallowed. My mouth was dry and my head felt like an orange that had been juiced. "I admit. I'm not thinking as clearly as usual."

"It's all right," he said, nearly a whisper. "You can count on me."

"I know." I leaned my head back, relaxing into him.

"The longer he's in there, with the food, all the weapons, and we're out here with nothing, the more advantage he gains. By shooting you, he thinks he's shortened that timeframe."

I was nodding, as though I were following, but really my head was banging like the bass at a Metallica concert.

"We need to go on the offensive right away."

"Offensive?" I sat up and spun around and looked at him. My vision blurred for a moment then refocused.

"How's your leg feel?"

"Like I got attacked by a meat grinder."

"Right," he said, his mind somewhere else.

"Dalton, you've got a plan already. I can see it in your eyes. What are you up to?"

His eyes met mine. Focused. Serious. Dalton the SEAL. "We need the satellite phone or a weapon or both. He's not coming out of that camp, but he's got to sleep some time. When he does, I'll slip through the electric fence and—"

"Wait," I said. "Why don't we get to the plane and call on the radio for help?"

"I thought of that." He frowned. "Remember how he wanted the plane in sight of camp?"

I nodded, following his train of thought. "He's got a long-range rifle. We try to get to the plane and he's got us. That and I suspect he's disabled the radio anyway."

"Really, why would—" *Damn.* I closed my eyes. *Damn!* "You think he already suspected us when I didn't shoot the bear."

"I'm not sure." He turned to face me. "I don't see how he could have gotten to the plane and back in time to catch us—"

"Yeah, I know. What were we thinking?"

He winced, turned away. "We can talk about that later. Right now we need to—"

"You think he disabled the radio when he anchored the plane then?" That seemed a stretch. "But that would mean—no, it had to be the kiss that gave us away."

"Anything's possible. I'm not sure what to think."

"But you're saying that the odds are, if you took the risk to try to swim out to the plane, in the dark, slowly so as not to be seen, if you actually made it without being hypothermic or getting shot, you'd find the radio disconnected."

He gave me a nod, satisfied I was following his logic. "That's what I would do. My gut tells me he didn't pull his weapon on a whim. He planned this. I'm not sure for how long, but when he left camp for the phone, he had something in mind."

"You think he planned to confront us? Get us to talk?"

"I don't know," he snapped. He stared down at the ground. "Like I said, what I do know is you're injured. The longer we let this go, without food, shelter, first-aid, the more vulnerable we'll be. Assuming the plane radio is disabled, that leaves only one option, infiltrating his camp. Tonight."

I nodded in agreement. He was right. We had no other choice.

"I want you to stay right here until I get back."

"Oh no," I said, shaking my head. "You're not going without me. Besides, your plan will never work. Look at you. You can't fit between the fence wires. It's got to be me. I'm small enough and flexible enough."

His eyebrows went up. Was that a hint of a blush? "Your leg isn't—"

"I'll be fine. Just"—I fiddled with my bandage—"tighten this thing up."

"You're not fine. You can't even walk."

"I can and I will. Besides, you said use it to our advantage, right? He won't suspect this. Maybe you should even let yourself be seen sneaking toward camp, keep his focus on you in case he's awake."

"It's too risky," Dalton said.

"Or what? It's not like we've got a lot of choices."

"We do have a choice. You stay here where you'll be safe. I'll wait until I'm sure he's asleep."

"Really? And what if something happens to you? Then what?" I whipped my hand into the air, blocking his rebuttal. "We work together. We're partners, right? That's how we get out of this. My strengths and yours. That's it."

He set his jaw. "You're wounded."

"I'm fine. You said it yourself, merely a flesh wound."

He stared at me a moment, a thoughtful expression in

his eyes. He was weighing the options. "You're going to be stubborn about this, aren't you?"

I gave him a grin.

"Fine. We'll do it just before dawn. But you need to show me you can walk on that leg before we go."

"Fine," I said and leaned back into his chest. "So what's the plan?"

"I'll approach the camp directly, on this line." He held his hand up, slicing through the air in the direction of the camp. "You'll circle around and approach from the backside. That's where you'll breach the perimeter. If it appears that he is alerted to your presence in any way, I'll create a distraction, rustle some alder branches or break some twigs, yell to him if I have to. If that happens, you run downhill, toward the lake and the cover of the pines, then at daybreak, circle back to rendezvous with me."

It was a good plan. Except for the running part. If I could actually walk on this leg, it would be a hobble. But I would make it work. I had to.

"Got it. Rustle, then rendezvous. But if not, once I'm inside the fence—"

"Once you're inside the fence, get to the plastic storage box. That's where the weapons and phone should be. Don't rush it."

I turned to look up at him. Our faces were inches apart. "One tip-toe at a time."

He grinned, that half-grin, the one that makes my tummy tingle and suddenly I wanted him to kiss me again.

"What is it?" he asked, his grin disappearing.

"What's what? Nothing." My eyes lingered on his lips. *Stop it.*

"Are you sure you want to do this?"

"Yes, of course. I just…yes. Go on."

His eyes held mine a moment, but then his expression

changed back to the serious SEAL. "If he hears you, duck behind the box. That way he can't be sure whether you have a weapon in your hand yet, which will buy you time. If that happens, or even if I see the slightest twitch, I'll clear the fence and—"

"I won't let it come to that."

He nodded, but I could tell, he wasn't convinced. "Once you've got something, weapon or phone, either one, get out of there. Don't get greedy."

"Hey, what's that supposed to mean?"

"It means we get in, get out, unnoticed, unharmed."

"Right," I said. Unharmed.

"What we're planning is risky. It could go south in an instant." He flashed a look of concern. "Are you sure you can get through the wires with that leg injury?"

I thought a moment. *No.* "Yes. I'm sure."

"Then all we do now is wait."

I leaned back against him and we sat in silence for awhile, listening to the sounds of the forest.

"Dalton?"

"Yeah?"

"You think I should have shot the bear."

Dalton pulled away from me, turned do we were face to face. "What? I didn't say that."

"But you did. You warned me about it."

He thought for a long moment before he answered. "I think you need to do what you think is right. Maybe shooting one bear to catch a poacher would save many bears. Maybe not. Maybe not shooting it made Rocky suspicious of us. Maybe not. Maybe it made no difference at all." His gaze shifted to the distance, the direction of Rocky. "The bear died regardless." He turned back to look at me, more intense now. "An unfortunate casualty."

"Is that what they teach you?"

He cocked his head to the side, confusion on his face. "What?"

"In SEAL school. In Afghanistan. Casualties are *unfortunate*, but an acceptable outcome of war. Is that the lesson I'm supposed to learn?"

"I don't know," he said, guarded.

"Is that what it means to be part of the team? To be a wildlife agent? I have to be a soldier? Why? Why does it have to be that way? Why do I have to compromise my values? Why can't I do it my way? Who makes the rules anyway? Who? Stan Martin? Maybe I don't want this job anyway. The hell with it."

"You don't mean that."

"I do. If it means what you're telling me. To save animals from harm, I have to become a killer myself. That's what you've been saying, right?"

"There's a difference," he said. "Sometimes it's justified."

"No," I said, shaking my head. "That's what people tell themselves. It's never justified. There's always another way."

"Not always. Unless you've been there, in that situation"— his voice changed, defensive—"you don't know."

"Sure. It's always about naive little Poppy. I don't play along. I don't follow the rules. All because I can't possibly *know*."

His expression turned dark and his eyes locked on me. "You don't know." There was pain in those eyes, the pain of regret.

Suddenly I realized I'd gone too far. I could see it clearly. "I'm sorry."

He narrowed his eyes at me then turned his face away from me.

"Was it in Afghanistan? Tell me what happened."

"We're not going to discuss my time in Afghanistan." He still wouldn't look at me.

"Okay," I said. "But you told me we're partners, that you

needed to be able to trust me, to know what I'd do. Well, I don't know about you. I don't know what you've done, what you're capable of. Where would you draw the line? What do you feel about—"

His head snapped back toward me. "What do you want me to say?" His stare held me in its grip. "I'm not you." He paused. "I'm a SEAL. Always will be."

I nodded. In a whisper, I said, "Kill or be killed."

The sky in the east was still dark, no hint of dawn. It was time. Now or never. My hands shook. Would my leg hold out?

As Dalton and I crept toward the camp, moving in an awkward crouch, I gripped my thigh, keeping pressure on the wound. It seemed to help with the pain, but I couldn't let Dalton see. He'd turn us back around. No way was I letting him take the risk alone. All this was my fault. And if he got shot, then where would we be?

This was my responsibility. I got us into this mess. I had to get us out.

Problem was, I wasn't sure how I was going to pull it off. The plan relied on Rocky being asleep. But he would have figured out this was our only option. He'd be waiting for us. But what else could we do?

With no cover but the dark of night, we pushed through the wet grass toward the glowing embers of the campfire. My heart beat a rhythm in my ear, the tempo increasing the closer we got.

Just get the phone. Or one gun. That's all I had to do. Get in, get out. Unnoticed, unharmed.

Rocky slouched in the chair, a long gun lying across his lap. Without binoculars, we couldn't be sure his eyes were closed, but, like Dalton said, everyone has to sleep sometime. Once you sit down, sleep will come, whether you want it to or not.

You could fall asleep standing up if you were tired enough.

Sitting in a chair, in the dark, in front of the warm fire, would put Rocky out at some point. At this hour, the odds were with us.

Once Dalton hunkered down in place, I crept around to my entry spot. My best approach was from behind Rocky. He might be a trained woodsman, even military, but he didn't have eyes in the back of his head.

My leg was beyond numb from all the walking, but it was still working, though I had to place my feet carefully, taking my time. One bad step, even a tiny stumble, might give me away.

The electrified wires surrounded the camp, four of them strung about ten to twelve inches apart. The lowest was about eight inches off the ground—too low to get under. I had to slip between that one and the next higher one, which meant I'd have to straddle it, putting my weight on my wounded leg. I drew in a breath. I could do it.

One last look at Rocky. He hadn't moved. He was asleep. He had to be.

I knelt in the cold, dewy grass and kicked my wounded leg back, swung it over, between the bottom two wires, kept my body long, then reached with my right arm and placed it on the ground inside. No problem. Easy yoga. I was straddling the wire. So far so good.

Now for the hard part. I leaned inward, shifting my weight to my bad leg, and lifted my other leg. Pain shot up my backside, but I held me leg in the air, breathing. *Okay. You can do this.* Getting my arm through first would be better. Then lean and roll. That should work.

Slowly, I lifted my outside arm. Almost there. As I pulled my arm through the wires, my coat shifted and my compass necklace dropped and hit the wire. Kazap! A jolt zipped through my body, seizing my muscles. I jerked upward and smacked the upper wire. Kazap! A groan of agony escaped my lips.

I froze, stuck between the wires, my eyes locked on Rocky in the chair, my heart jackhammering inside my chest.

I huffed, trying to settle my nerves. *Breathe. Breathe. You can do this. Just stay still.* Maybe I hadn't woken him. I waited, my back arched, between the wires, one leg in, one leg out. The necklace dangled from my neck, inches from the wire. Slowly, I shifted my weight to my good leg, reached up and tucked the charm into my mouth to get it away from the wire.

I turned my head back to check on Rocky. "Well, whaddaya know," he said, calmly looking over his shoulder. "The brave little rabbit's come right into the fox's den."

Shit! I rolled out of the wires, hitting the back of my hand on the upper one, giving me one more jolt. I pulled myself to my feet and stumbled into the dark night.

"Run, little rabbit. Run!" Rocky shouted after me followed by a laugh that sent a shiver through to my bones.

Chapter 12

I ran into a veil of pitch dark as fast as my bum leg would take me, down the hill, into the pines. I kept running. The laughter faded behind me, but no gunshots. He didn't follow. But still, I had to get away. Something about that laugh frightened me to my core.

Finally, I came across a fallen log and slumped down next to it. Running in the dark was dangerous. I would catch my breath, wait for dawn, then circle back to the rendezvous location.

Adrenaline zipped through my veins—the ultimate drug. My leg didn't hurt, I didn't feel the cold, and my brain shifted into overdrive.

I snugged my coat tight around my neck. *That laugh.* He wasn't alarmed or worried. He was amused. I don't know what I'd been thinking, trying to talk to him. When he caught us kissing, he could have kept up the guide act, keeping it legal, without risking anything. We had no hard evidence against him. Yet he pulled his gun. It didn't make sense. What was Rocky thinking?

Put yourself in his shoes, my dad would say. Why would Rocky pull his sidearm on Dalton, then shoot me in the leg, but not shoot just now, when I was right in front of him again? None of this made any sense. Had I startled him awake and he didn't think to shoot until I was out of sight? No, he'd shouted for me to run. As if he were actually cheering me on, wanting me to get away. But why?

The eastern sky showed no sign of the sun, so I hunkered down. Wandering in the wilderness in the dark was not a good idea. Everyone worries about nocturnal predators, but no one thinks of the more common dangers, like getting stuck in the eye by a branch. Yep. Better to stay put until dawn.

In autumn, the Alaskan woods are quiet, peaceful. So unlike the jungle, where the night sounds are louder than the day. If Rocky decided to follow me, I'd hear him coming.

When the sun finally arrived, a light rain started to fall. *Great*. The bandage around my thigh had come loose. Fresh blood oozed down my leg, mingling with the dark, gooey dried stuff. My thigh was swollen and red. I winced as I tightened the bandage then got to my feet. I had to get back to Dalton.

I pushed through the thicket and a patch of devil's club, avoiding the spiny barbs that line the stems and undersides of their massive leaves. There was a rustle ahead. I dropped to my knees. Waiting, hidden. There it was again. Rocky wouldn't be that careless. Not to make that kind of noise. Easy now, I slowly rose to my feet.

About twenty yards away stood a bull moose, staring at me, stone-still save for the sideways slide of his jaw, crunching branches with his teeth. His rack must have been at least a sixty inch spread with sharp tines. The massive antlers looked like thorny paddles. Absolutely majestic. He sized me up as I sized him up, two beings meeting unexpectedly in the woods.

I've seen moose before, but to face off with one, alone, made my knees weak. God he was huge. A half ton of muscle and, this time of year, oozing with testosterone. At the shoulder he stood taller than me, probably six feet. He took a step, shifted his gaze, turning slightly to the side, showing his flank. The flap of skin hanging from his chin, the bell I thought it was called, swung with his movement.

"Okay, moose. I'm backing away," I said in a calm, soothing voice. "I'm backing away."

His ears perked up, twitched. One of them turned to the side. His tongue flicked in and out, licking his lips like a cow. He took a couple more steps toward me, a moose mosey, tilting his head back and forth, ever so slightly, causing his huge antlers to swing side to side.

"Look at you," I said, letting my mouth spit out whatever words came to mind as I slowly stepped backward. "All handsome, big boy. I'm going to back away, okay? I don't want any trouble."

Drawing his head back, he snorted, his breath a tiny cloud of mist in the cold air. He looked like he was posing for a National Geographic photo, though his fur was matted from the rain.

"That's okay. I'm having a bad hair day, too, my friend."

I took another step back, my foot caught on a root, and my bad leg gave. I stumbled and crashed into some brush.

The moose jumped backward and spun around, his hind side facing me now.

I managed to get back to my feet, but not without a scrape across my face. Warm blood ran down my cheek.

The moose watched over his shoulder with wary eyes. My eyes fixed on the massive hump on his back, pure muscle to power his front legs. He could run thirty-five miles an hour, knocking down half the forest as he went. He might not have the sharp canines of a bear or wolf, but that rack on his head could gouge with the force of a bulldozer.

His eyes intent on me now, he slowly turned and walked toward me, one carefully placed hoof at a time.

"Nothing to see here, Mr. Moose. Just a klutzy woman with a bum leg. Nothing to be alarmed about. I'll be running along now. See you later, then."

He came to a halt, his fur standing up, ears pinned back, and his head dropped low. With a snort, his front legs slapped at the ground and he charged.

Holy shit!

I ducked behind two trees as his antlers rammed the trunks. *Crash!*

I stepped right. He reared back and plowed into the trees again. I shifted left and staggered to another tree, spun around it, turning in another direction. He was right behind me. The crack of his antlers smacking the tree ripped through the forest. I lunged toward the next tree, thrashing through a patch of devil's club, and spun around. The moose backed away and took off into the brush.

My heart hammered in my chest. I huffed and huffed, trying to catch my breath. *Damn, that was close.*

My head spun. I sat down in the moss. "Damn," I said out loud.

All right, McVie. You're all right.

My face burned, all the way down my neck. I reached up and felt the thorns stuck in my skin from the devil's club. *Great. Just great.*

Fresh blood soaked my pant leg. The bandage had come loose again. I tried to tighten it, but my hands were shaking. *Dammit!*

Deep breath. I worked the ends of the bandage and managed to get the bleeding to stop, but I'd ripped it open and made it worse.

I looked around. Nothing but the forest deep.

Dalton's voice echoed in my head, *Bear gets your scent, he won't look so cuddly.*

I got to my feet again. Now, which way was north? I hobbled downward, toward the lake. From there, I'd get my bearings.

It's this way. No, that way.

I sat down. My head dizzy. I needed to rest. Just for a minute. It was cold. So cold. My teeth were chattering.

I need to keep moving.

The rain was coming down harder now, feeling like pellets stinging my face. The pattering turned to a steady whoosh as it penetrated the canopy. Droplets ran down my neck. My rain hat hung on my back, the cord tight at my throat, rubbing on the rash where I had fallen against the devil's club. I slung it up atop my head, cinched down the chin strap, and drew in a long breath. *Which way?*

The forest in every direction was dark and misty. I couldn't see the sun to gauge direction. All right. The downward slope headed for the lake. That meant I needed to stay at this level for five hundred yards or so. Not go up or down. That would take me on a course to circle back to Dalton. I could do this.

Putting one foot in front of the other, over moss-covered logs, through the blueberry bushes, across a patch of skunk cabbage, I went. What was a little dizziness? I could see. I could find my way.

I could do it on my own. Alone.

Alone.

Maybe Martin had been right. This alone crap was overrated. My hand went to the compass necklace at my neck. *Oh Chris. I'm so sorry. I didn't mean to make things worse. I'll make it up to you, I swear.*

I laughed out loud. I was holding a fake little compass. *Oh Chris. If you only knew. I* have *lost my way.*

Every part of the forest dripped water. My pants were soaked. My socks sloshed in my boots. My hair was heavy on my back. I should've been freezing. But I wasn't.

Is that what happened when you became hypothermic? You no longer felt cold. Yes. I remember. Then a feeling of well-being, euphoria even. Was I shivering? No. Wasn't that what happened?

My leg must have been dragging. It caught on a stick and I collapsed to the ground.

Must get up.

Dalton can't be far.

I planted my hands on the earth and pushed myself upright. One step. Another step.

I was back on the ground again, my face in the moss. It felt soft. Nice.

I could sleep.

"Thank God I found you." A face, inches from mine. "I've been worried sick."

I tried to open my eyes.

"Are you all right? Poppy? Talk to me."

The throbbing of my head brought me around. I was in Alaska. In the woods.

"What happened?" he asked.

Dalton. That was his name. I tried to sit up, but my head spun. A wave of nausea came over me and I leaned over and retched.

He held my hair back, then pulled me to him. "You've gotten too cold," he said, wrapping his arms around me. "Dammit, I shouldn't have let you go."

I remember. The bush plane. The lodge. Joe smoking that cigar.

"No cigars."

A bear. Charging toward me. *I won't shoot. I can't shoot.*

"Poppy. Poppy! C'mon, stay with me."

Dalton. A kiss. "Rocky gun. Run. Run."

"Here, drink some water."

He held a plastic bag at my mouth. I drank.

"There now," he said. "Just rest. Get warm."

Dalton. Holding me. Warm now.

I blinked my eyes open. Dalton was holding me tight.

"You feeling better?"

I nodded. "Did I sleep?" My arms felt heavy.

"Yeah." His hand went to my forehead. "How are you feeling?"

"Better, I think."

He smoothed my hair back from my face, plucked a couple twigs from it. "What the hell happened?"

Was it dark already again?

"Poppy? Tell me what happened."

"You wouldn't believe me if I told you."

"Looks like you got into the devil's club."

My hand went to my neck. "Yeah. I could use some tweezers."

"I'll help. I didn't want to do it while you were asleep and risk waking you."

I nodded in understanding.

"Let's see that leg first." He pulled back the bandage and winced.

"That bad, huh?"

He gave me a reassuring smile. "I've seen worse. A little bleeding is good. Flushes it out."

"Right," I said. He was a bad liar.

He took hold of my chin to turn my head and get a good look at the thorns in my neck. "You just can't keep yourself out of trouble, can you?" He was trying to sound funny, keep it light, keep my spirits up, but it fell flat.

"Just get them out."

"All right. Hold still."

With the patience of a neurosurgeon, he carefully plucked away while intermittently scanning behind me for any sign of Rocky. "So who made the first move? You or the plant?"

He said it with such a serious tone, a smile crept across my face.

"It was a moose, actually. I tried to back away, but he charged."

Dalton sat back, his eyebrows up. "You're kidding."

I nodded. "Scared the living shit out of me."

He pulled another thorn. "I bet."

"Nothing more badass in these woods than a bull moose all doped up on testosterone."

He gave me a frown. "I don't know about that."

"Ow!" I pulled away.

"Sorry," he whispered.

"Seriously, a moose in rut can—"

"Rocky," he said, serious now. "He let you run away."

"I told you. I knew it. He doesn't want to kill us. We should try talking to him again."

Dalton was shaking his head before I finished the sentence. "No. Don't you see? He let you go. All the while he was scanning for me."

"What? You think he sees only you as a real threat? I'm going to try not to be insulted by that. But it only makes my point. *I'll* go talk to him."

"No," he said, more sternly than usual. "Listen to me. He could leave. He could go get in the plane right now and go. Leave us to die. Why hasn't he?"

"Because, like I said, he's no killer. He's got to make a point." I couldn't possibly sound convincing. I wasn't sure myself.

"Okay, but he could send someone else to get us later. Leave us out here for a while. That would make a point."

"He could I suppose, but he'd be vulnerable getting to the plane, leaving the camp. We could ambush him."

"Not really that risky. He has all the weapons. We have none. We've been out in the cold for two nights. We're tired. You're wounded."

"Okay, so maybe he's scared. Maybe he's not able to assess the situation as rationally as you can."

"No. He's smart. And arrogant. Didn't you hear him laughing?"

I nodded. That was some creepy laughing.

"No,"—he shook his head—"there's another reason." He examined my neck. He'd pulled the last of the thorns. "Wait here," he said and went into the woods. He came back with a leaf from the devil's club plant, crushed it in his hands. "This should soothe the burn," he said. "As ironic as that may be." He gently rubbed it on my neck.

"Dalton, what are you saying? What other reason?"

"It's not me he's focused on. To him, I'm a dopey boy from Oklahoma. Boring. Inconsequential. But you. Little Miss Sharpshooter. All cocky and capable and sexy as hell." He paused. "I mean, what man wouldn't want to—"

"Are you saying this is all about him having the hots for me? About him trying to impress me?" No way. That didn't make sense either.

"I'm saying he isn't your everyday trafficker, selling buckskins out of his trunk. Who knows what he did in the lower forty-eight. Maybe he's a felon. Maybe he didn't fit in. Maybe he just couldn't quite get his shit together. Snubbed by the ladies. Couldn't keep a job. Who knows. But I do know one thing. We shouldn't underestimate how dangerous he is. This isn't like Ray Goldman."

"What? Ray Goldman was on our most-wanted list."

"Yeah, because orcas are high profile animals. But Ray was a fisherman. Yes, you saw him as a kidnapper, a killer. But in his own mind, he was just another fisherman." Dalton looked around, over his shoulder, then back at me, frowning. "With Rocky, it's different." His face took on a shadow of concern. "For him, it's all about the hunt."

My stomach dropped and the cold air seemed to envelope

me. "Are you saying—?"

"I'm saying that out here, for Rocky, it's a whole different world. Out here he's in his element. Out here, he's the apex predator." Dalton looked me square in the eyes. "And you're a little rabbit."

My whole body went cold. Dalton was right.

Chapter 13

My palms got sweaty and my head light. "This isn't good," I said. "Not. Good."

Dalton watched me, letting it sink in.

"I can't believe I got us into this. I should've known. I should have seen. Back at the lodge. He heard us talking that night. Or, I don't know, what I said to Townsend about him. He seemed so meek, so nerdy. Who would've thought? I mean, he wouldn't even make eye contact. I figured he—or maybe he…maybe he didn't suspect us at all." I looked Dalton in the eyes. "If I hadn't kissed you and—"

"What? No." He sighed. "This isn't your fault." He turned away, his jaw tight. "It's mine. I should've known better."

What? You mean you didn't want—

Dalton jerked his head to the left. He'd heard something.

"What is it?" I whispered.

"Dammit," he said, his eyes now on the sky.

Then I heard it too. The drone.

"Get him to focus on you," Dalton said.

I had a pretty good idea what Dalton was thinking. I got to my feet and stormed toward the drone, my fists in the air, shouting at it. A crazed woman was not a character I had to fake right now.

The drone dropped nearly to my level and hovered about twenty yards away.

I stumbled, for effect, then bent over and propped my hand on my hip as though I were trying to catch my breath.

Bam! A rock slammed into the drone, knocking it sideways. The propellers made a grinding noise. Another rock flew by my head but missed the drone this time. It sputtered and shot skyward, tilting to the side, but managed to stay airborne.

I swung around. "Hit it again!"

Dalton threw another rock, but the drone was too far away.

"You damaged it," I said with a whoop.

"C'mon," Dalton said. "Let's get out of sight anyway. It'll be dark soon."

I limped after him, into the cover of the pines.

Dalton found a dry patch of moss under a rocky overhang. "Right here," he said and gestured for me to lie down.

"But we're barely a hundred yards from where he saw us."

"It's all right. He'll assume we ran."

I eyed Dalton, skeptical.

"Trust me."

I nodded and dropped to my knees to crawl into the mossy bed.

"What do we do now?" I asked once he sat down.

"We give him what he wants." He frowned and looked me in the eye. "At least make him think it."

"What he wants? You mean use me as bait." I closed my eyes. I didn't know if I had the energy to hear his plan, let alone enact it.

"No," he said, shaking his head. "Like I said, he doesn't find me so...intriguing."

My head was in some kind of fog. "I don't understand."

"I need some things from the plane."

"The plane? You're going out there? To the plane? But you said—"

He gave me the I'm-doing-this-no-matter-what look. "We wait for darkness. Then I'm going to the plane. There were some things in the back. I'll check the radio too, but you and I both know he's disabled it."

"What do you mean, things? What are you planning to do?"

"You stay here. Keep warm and try to get some sleep."

"What? You can't be serious."

"Listen to me. You need to rest. That's the best way. I know you. I know you'll fight until you collapse. But right now, you need to trust me. We're a team. Partners. Do you understand?"

I crossed my arms. "You're planning something and keeping me out of it."

"It's not that. We need to know what resources we have. The plane might give us some options. It's worth the risk. I need to see what is there, then we'll work out the details. For that, I'm going to need you at your best. That means rest now." His eyes pleaded for me to consent. "Tell me you will."

He was right about needing to rest. My leg throbbed. My head throbbed. My neck burned. I was cold and wet. And I was pissed. Was I even thinking clearly? But for him to swim out to the plane? Alone? In the dark? What did he think he'd find that was that valuable? Was he not telling me something or were we that desperate?

I held my hand to my head. I wasn't sure. Somehow I couldn't concentrate. "Okay," I said. "If you think it's our best option, but…Dalton?" Man, I was tired. "Do you really think we'll get out of this alive?"

His eyes shifted to his hands. "We're smart. We're well trained."

"But?" I could feel it. There was definitely a but.

"There's something about this guy. This doesn't feel right. This whole thing. It's not about him being a poacher."

I nodded. "In Costa Rica, we knew what we were up against. In Norway too. This feels…" I shook my head.

"Yeah."

"In Costa Rica, when Chris—" I sighed. *Oh Chris*. All the feelings of guilt rushed in. "He risked his life for me, my job. And now I don't know if I'll ever..."

"Don't say it."

"I put his job on the line. He could get fired for what I did. That was stupid."

"You were sticking up for him."

"Yeah, but he was right. You were right. I wasn't thinking. And now...this."

"You've been friends all these years. He knows who you are. I'm sure he's already forgiven you."

"You're probably right. Because he's Chris. That doesn't mean it's forgivable."

Dalton squeezed my hand. "When we get back, you'll call him, tell him how you feel."

I nodded. "If we get back."

"We'll get through this. You got me?"

My stomach ached, my leg hurt like hell, and we were stranded in the center of the wilderness with nothing. Nothing but each other. I nodded.

"You should get some rest," he said.

"Yeah, right. There's no way I'm going to be able to sleep."

Dalton nodded in understanding. "Tell me about Chris. How'd you two meet anyway?"

"Well, the first time was in sixth grade. My mom was stationed in the Philippines. Up to that point, I'd been homeschooled by my dad, since we moved around so much, but she'd decided I was old enough to go to school with the other kids at that age, I guess.

"For several months, I endured it, bored. Then Chris showed up in class one day, sat down beside me, and the first words out of his mouth were, 'Hey, wanna be best friends?' Kids were always coming and going. The nature of being a Navy brat. If you wanted a friend, you connected quickly. I said sure and that was that.

"I think at the time, what I liked so much about him was that he seemed exotic. It was his skin, his hair. All the other kids were so plain. And boring."

I chewed on my lower lip. "I know it sounds awful, but I always had a hard time getting along with other girls. All they ever wanted to talk about was boys. How they should wear their hair, for the boys. What clothes to wear, to attract the boys. Which girls were dating which boys. With Chris, it was different. I didn't have to deal with all that stuff because he was a boy. We worried about world politics, about the environment, about national debt. We'd stay up all night talking about religion.

"Then one day, at lunch time, a couple of boys cornered us. Bullies. They started in calling me Pippity-poppity-poo and—"

"What?" Dalton grinned. "They called you Pippity—"

"Don't even," I said. "Do you want to hear the story or not?"

"I do."

"So these boys, who I wasn't exactly fond of, get us in this corner and start in, calling Chris names. Well, I wasn't having it. I realized, in that moment, that I'd started thinking of Chris as my boyfriend." I smiled at the memory. "And they were calling him names like...well, you know.

"One boy, Tommy was his name, I'll never forget, he got right in Chris's face. I grabbed him by the shoulder, spun him around, and punched him right in the nose. Blood everywhere. 'You don't talk to my boyfriend like that,' I shouted.

"The boys ran away. I thought I'd really done something, all proud of myself for sticking up for him. But Chris stood there, shaking his head, tears in his eyes. He was angry. With me.

'I'm not your boyfriend,' he said and stomped away, leaving me there with bloody knuckles."

"Wow," Dalton said. "Then what happened?"

I stared at him, into those eyes. Is that what was happening now? Did I completely misread Dalton's intentions? Was he just trying to be a kind partner and then I went and kissed him? I turned away. What had I been thinking?

"What happened next?" he nudged.

"My dad lectured me on why he'd gotten me all those Kuntaw lessons in the first place. You know, the Filipino martial art I used to knock you on your ass that day we first met."

"Yeah, I remember," he said with a frown.

"He said I was supposed to learn discipline. Not beat up the boys."

Dalton laughed. "Right. Guess you haven't mastered that one yet."

I grinned.

"I meant, what happened with Chris."

"He wouldn't talk to me. Two months later, my mom got transferred. I thought I'd never see him again. Then, several years later, he walked into my high school classroom in California. By then he'd come out and everything was clear, as if it had sorted itself out. We've been best friends ever since.

"Oh Dalton, what if I never see him—"

"You will." He squeezed my hand again. "You will. Trust me."

Dusk had descended on the forest, taking all color, leaving nothing but darkness.

He took off his coat, pulled me tight to him, then wrapped the coat around me like blanket. "You need to stay warm. Right now, the most important thing is that you get a good night's sleep."

I melted into his chest. I might have misread that kiss, but I could trust Dalton. With my life.

I awoke with a start. Someone was near.

"It's me," Dalton whispered. "It's all right. It's just me."

I glanced around. Daylight had filled the forest once again. "What happened? I must have—"

"Slept, yes. You needed it."

"But I, you—" Dalton stood next to a pile of things—things he'd gotten from the plane. "You've already gone?" I shook my head in disbelief.

"Did you know you snore?"

My mouth dropped open.

"I'm just kidding." He winked at me. "I made sure you were safe. You needed the rest. And I got some things."

There were parts of the airplane seat, straps and cords, a duffle bag, and an old iron bear trap lying in a pile.

"You swam to the plane? You must be freezing." He'd left his coat wrapped around me. I got to my feet and held it out to him. "Get your coat on."

"I'm fine."

"You're naked." From the waist up, which was enough to distract me. "We don't need you getting hypothermic too. Now put it on."

He took it from me, but first held his hand to my forehead and checked my pupils, giving me a nod of approval.

"So what's your plan? What are you going to do with all this?" I pointed to the trap. "Do you think he'll just step into that?"

"No. You're going to have to lure him into it."

"Lure him? *I'm* going to lure him? And what about you?"

"Oh, I'll be dead."

My head felt a little better, but did he just say—"Come again?"

"There's only one way he's coming out of that fortress he's built. If I'm dead." He held a seat cushion he'd pulled from the plane up to his chest and knocked on the metal backing. "This ought to do it."

"You can't be serious. Your plan is to use a seat cushion for a bullet-proof vest? Are you nuts? He has a high-powered rifle. You can't be sure that will stop the bullet."

"You're right. I can't be sure. But it's the best we've got."

"No, no." I sliced at the air with my hands. "No! We'll talk to him again. We'll find another way."

Dalton put his hands on my shoulders. "Poppy, there is no other way." His eyes held mine. "You know it."

"The radio?"

"Disabled. Just as we thought." He looked at me with those eyes. "He planned this. From the beginning."

"But you can't—"

"Listen to me. We have one shot at this. One. Do you understand?"

I spun around and sat down. This couldn't be happening. Dalton was going to put himself in the line of fire, with a seat cushion for protection. This wasn't happening. I shook my head. "It's too risky."

"I know. Just like in Norway and Costa Rica. Only this time I'm taking the lead." He gave me a gentle shrug. "It's my turn, right?"

I shook my head.

"It's our only chance. We've got to take him by surprise. A full-on, frontal attack would be suicide."

I nodded. I knew he was right. But, what if—?

"We're going to set the trap. Then go down by the log that crosses the river. It's the only place to cross and he can see us from the camp. He'll think we've gotten desperate. That's where he'll shoot me."

I was shaking my head again. "No. No."

"As soon as he sees me fall, he'll come out. He'll want to verify the kill."

"What if you really get shot? What if he shoots you in the head?"

"He won't. SEALs are trained to take a chest shot."

"But you said he wasn't really a SEAL. What if—?"

"You don't worry about me. Think only of taking care of yourself. Do you understand? And stick to the plan. Like the SEALs, live and die by the plan."

"Exactly!" I shook my head. "I can't believe this is our plan."

"When you get to the trap, don't hesitate, don't look at it, run over it, as fast as you can. Go way beyond it. If you hesitate, if you check, you'll give me away."

"What do you mean?" He'd lost me.

He picked up the trap. "It's broken. I'm going to have to trip it. That means you've got to keep him busy until I can circle back around and get into position."

"Are you kidding?"

His stare was heavy.

"What if he doesn't step into it? How will—?"

"We are going to put it in a place where he'll have to step in it. You'll step in it. He'll follow."

"How do you know he's not going to just shoot me?"

Dalton's eyes turned dark. He looked away. "I don't."

My stomach dropped. "This is crazy."

"It's a good plan." A beat. "Considering the circumstances."

I ran my fingers through my hair, tried to make my brain settle down and think.

Dalton stared at his hands. "He wants to hunt you. I feel it. In my bones. He's going to track you."

"What if you're right and he shoots? What if you actually get shot? What if he kills you? Then what happens?"

Dalton stood, picked up the trap. "Then let's hope I'm wrong about him."

Chapter 14

Dalton chose a muddy spot in a tiny stream to hide the trap. He tied a cord to the broken lever that tripped it and ran it into the tall grass on the edge, then crawled on his belly into the weeds. "Can you see me?"

"No. Not really."

"Is that a no or a not really?"

"It's good. He'll be running right? It's good."

Dalton crawled back out. "All right, then. It's showtime." He held the seat cushion to his chest and had me help him strap it tight, then the other on his back. He'd stuffed a pair of pants he'd found in the plane with pine needles. "This is going to work," he said. "He'll think I'm floating face down. You'll keep him busy for at least an hour. Time for me to get out of the water without being seen, then back here and hidden. You can do that, right?"

"I don't know." I shook my head again. I couldn't let him go out there with only a seat cushion for protection. This was crazy.

"We've been over this." His eyes locked on me. "Promise me."

I couldn't.

"Listen to me. This will only work if we're both all in, one hundred percent. And it will work. You just have to trust me."

What could I say? What could I do? He was right. We were out of options. I nodded. "I promise."

He gave me a smile. "It will be all be over soon."

"I know, I—" That's what I was afraid of. "Dalton, I...this whole thing...and you and me...I can't go without knowing..." I looked into his eyes and the words fell away.

With a gentle smile, he said, "Knowing what?"

"I need to know..." *Damn.* My cheeks were on fire. *You kissed me and then—* He was staring, waiting. "Your first name." *Oh geez. I'm a total dope.*

"That's what you want?" he said with a hint of disappointment. He shook his head to blow it off.

"I just thought, you know, since we've been working together, and then all this, that we'd, well, you know, you're my partner and I don't even know your name, so I thought that, you know, in case everything—"

He grinned. "You're babbling."

"What?" I drew back, thrown off. "I don't babble."

His eyebrows went up.

"It's just that I don't understand. You don't want me to know because you're embarrassed?"

"No, that's not it. I just—" He gave me a resigned grin. "It's Garrett."

I smiled. "Garrett. That's a fine name."

He rolled his eyes and turned away.

"What? I mean it. Really. What's wrong with Garrett?"

He shook his head. "Nothing. Except when you were named after your mom's favorite movie character and your mom was—well, how lame is that?"

Obviously there was a lot more to it, but now wasn't the time. "I'm still going to call you Dalton because—"

"Yes,"—he nodded—"yes, you are."

Our eyes locked in an uncomfortable moment. "That is, if I still have a job," I managed. "And, you know."

"Don't worry about that now," he finally said. "Focus on our mission here. On the plan. Okay?"

I nodded. Staying alive. I could focus on that.

He smiled. "Okay, let's get going."

"Hold on," I said. "I need one more moment." I drew in a deep breath.

He took hold of my hand, pulled me closer to him, and looked into my eyes. "It's all right," he whispered. "It will be all right."

I wrapped my arms around him and didn't want to let go.

"It's a good plan," he murmured in my ear.

Ak-ak-ak rattled behind me.

I pushed away from him with a start. Spun around. A raven. It was a raven.

My chest heaved, trying to get my breath to return. I came back around to Dalton. Our eyes met for a brief moment then he continued scanning. His muscles pulled tight, on full alert.

"It was just a bird," I said.

He nodded. "Still," he said. "We should get moving."

I drew in a breath, then another, trying to get my racing heart to settle. "Yeah."

We moved along the ridge, keeping at a low crouch, until we came within about a hundred yards of the log bridge. From there, we let ourselves be seen, a head up here, a push through the branches there, as though we were trying our best to stay hidden. Dalton stayed clear. Mainly I was the one exposing myself, betting that Dalton was right and Rocky wouldn't shoot me. Shoot to kill anyway.

Dalton came to a halt and peered through some brush. I crawled up next to him. "Has he noticed?"

Dalton nodded. "He's got the binoculars sighted on us."

"And he hasn't shot me again. That's a good sign I guess."

"You ready?" he asked with an encouraging nod.

Deep breath. I nodded.

Dalton took off at a quick pace, running for the log. I was right on his tail, staying between him and Rocky, blocking any chance of a shot until he was out on the log. He had to be directly above the river before we allowed Rocky an opening. Five more strides and we'd be there.

One, two, three. Dalton was on the log. I feigned a stumble, making a space between us. Ca-rack! The shot reverberated across the distance, then the clang of a bullet hitting metal. I dropped to my knees. God, I hoped Rocky hadn't heard it at that distance.

Dalton crumpled into a heap, then slumped over.

"Dalton!"

He didn't turn. Didn't say anything. Didn't give me any sign he was okay.

"Dalton!"

He slid from the log and plummeted to the river below. I spun around. Rocky already had the binoculars to his eyes, watching. I looked back to Dalton. He floated in a froth of white water, face down. Had he really been hit? *Oh god!* I couldn't see his face, couldn't see if he was conscious. "Dalton!"

Could he hear me over the rumble of the rapids? With his ears in the water? "Dalton!" His body bobbed in the rapids like a fallen log, farther and farther away from me. "Dal-ton!"

Oh my god! What if he was really shot? I couldn't breathe. Couldn't think. *What were we thinking?*

Okay. Deep breath. Of course he wouldn't give me a sign. Rocky might see it. He had to play it out. Be convincing. To the end. Dalton always, always stayed in character.

He's all right. Stick to the plan. The plan.

The white rush of water carried him toward the lake. Part of the plan.

I spun back around. Rocky was wasting no time. He had the

lid of the plastic storage box flipped open and was gearing up. Dalton had been right. Rocky was leaving camp to confirm the kill.

I bolted from the log and ran for cover, back to the spot from which Dalton had been watching Rocky. I burrowed in and crawled on my elbows to get a view, my chest heaving.

This is happening. My hands shook. I had skills. But that man was fully armed, well fed and rested. I had to keep him occupied, on my trail, but not let him catch me. All that, exhausted, wounded, recovering from hypothermia. It was going to take everything I had.

Dalton, you better be at the trap when we get there.

I drew in a deep breath and moved to higher ground.

CHAPTER 15

Rocky passed through the gate of the camp fully loaded—handgun at his belt, pack on his back, rifle slung over his shoulder, and the crossbow in his hand. He covered the ground from camp to the river's edge at the speed of a cheetah, I swear. How was I going to stay ahead of him?

He went straight to the log, then followed the rim of the gorge downhill, his eyes trained on the water, scanning. I saw before he did. Dalton's body—or fake body—floating out in the lake. Even from where I was hidden, I could see his coat spread on the surface, the legs floating behind. He'd made a good, believable dummy. *Unless?—Don't go there.*

Rocky moved double time toward the lake. By now, the dummy was nearly a hundred yards out from shore. Rocky came to a halt, set down his crossbow, and dropped his backpack. He slowly turned around, scanning the hillside. I dropped down, my heart racing.

For a moment, I thought he was going to strip down and swim out to the body for confirmation. If he did, he'd have to leave all his weapons unattended on shore. Could I get there in time? Grab his gun and this would all be over?

He stood there, as though seriously considering the swim, then pulled the binoculars from his pack. A flush of nerves made me shiver. Would Dalton's pine needle-stuffed pants hold up to scrutiny?

Rocky held the binoculars to his eyes for too long. Surely he saw it was a fake. *Oh, what if it isn't?* Then he lowered the glasses and turned back in my direction. I swear his steely eyes zeroed right in on me and my breath caught in my throat.

"Where are you, little rabbit?" His voice thundered across the distance with a rough edge to it. Different now. Heavy with thirst. "Where have you run?"

I set my teeth. *Game on, asshole.*

I leapt to my feet, sure he'd see me. *C'mon. I'm right up here, you creep.* I limped along the ridge, glancing back to be sure he was following but still some distance away. Whatever it took—circling back, zigzagging, staying uphill—I needed to keep track of where he was and not let him get too close while I killed the time needed for Dalton to get to the trap and be ready.

If he was alive.

This is a bad plan, a terrible plan—no. Dalton was alive when he went into the river. Wasn't he? *Knock it off. Just stick to the plan. Lure Rocky to the trap. Dalton will be there.*

At the far side of the ridge I pushed through a thicket. A covey of ptarmigan lifted off with a clatter, wings thrashing through the brush. My heart leapt into my throat.

"Careful, there, little rabbit," Rocky shouted.

I spun around. He was much closer than I'd thought. How could that be?

"You'll give yourself away," he warned.

Shit! I dropped my head and ran, bounding over the rocky terrain, dodging bushes. Tiny twigs slapped me in the face as I headed toward the pines and the deep forest. I needed the cover, where I could get ahead of him, then I'd circle back.

I leaped over a rock, my leg faltered, and I went down, slamming my chin into the ground. The fall knocked the wind out of me. I pushed up onto my hands and knees, my chest heaving.

Rocky's laughter rumbled after me, so close it felt like he was breathing down my neck.

I got back to my feet, stumbled forward, but managed to get going again. Maybe I could hide. I could duck under a bush, let him pass me by, then turn and head back the way we'd come. His speed and mine, in opposite directions, would put more space between us. Yes, that was what I'd do. Leave a false trail, then circle back.

He might be a good tracker, but I had some skills too. But did I have time? Was he too close?

As I entered the thick of the forest, I snapped a little sapling in two with my boot, then four paces later a pine branch, then in another ten feet, I left a scuff in the wet soil. I crept sideways then, making sure to leave no sign and circled back and got down on my belly in the mud and crawled under a moss-covered log.

As I lay still, my heartbeat thrummed in my chest sending pulses of throbbing pain through my leg. I focused on my breathing, trying to settle it as I waited.

Then he was there. Without a sound he appeared like a ghost. *God he's fast.*

My heartbeat thundered in my ears, racing back up to double time.

Through the foliage I could see he'd stopped to examine the sapling. He sniffed the air, like a dog, then turned to scan the forest behind him. As he came around, his eyes cast on me. I shrank back, holding my breath, sure he'd seen me. But his eyes kept scanning at a steady pace.

He moved forward a few steps, holding the crossbow up at the ready. He took the broken pine branch in his hand and twirled it between his fingers. A few more feet and he stopped. He squatted down, pushed back the plants around the scuff I'd left, then rose, looking in the direction I'd intended for him to continue. He paused, scanning again.

Go on. That's the way.

His feet planted, shoulder width apart. *Oh crap. He sees me.* Then I heard the zip of his fly. Then the patter of urine hitting the forest floor.

His feet swiveled as he tucked himself back inside his pants and zipped up again.

He finally moved forward, without a sound.

I let out my breath. Another thirty seconds passed before I slipped from under the log and hobbled back toward the river.

It wouldn't be long before he'd realize I'd fooled him. Once he'd walked a bit without seeing any sign, he'd circle back. By then, I'd be over the hillside and headed toward the trap.

I ran along the same path I'd taken down, where he'd followed, so that my tracks would be somewhat hidden amid his. I didn't need him finding me again so soon.

I pushed through the brush, staying low, moving as fast as I could with my hand on my leg and careful not to twist an ankle over the rocky ground.

When I got to the thicket where I'd flushed the ptarmigan, Rocky's voice stopped me dead in my tracks. "You are a sly one."

I spun around, my heart racing. Where was he?

Up, to the left? On the ridge above me? How had he made it that far back already?

I dropped to my hands and knees. A groan escaped my lips as searing pain shot through my hip. I gripped my wound and crawled through the thicket.

"He had to go, you know." His voice made me duck lower. "I couldn't let him get between you and me."

How far was he? Too close. *I let him get too close.* My pulse hammered away in my ears.

He's going to kill me. I'm going to die. Out here. Alone.

No. Stop it. He's taunting you. That's good. Part of the plan.

He was confident he'd killed Dalton. Good. All was going as Dalton had planned.

So why am I shaking like a...like a little rabbit?

"It's just you and me now, babe."

He'd moved. Circling me. But how far away was he now? I could make a run for it. Maybe.

"And we're going to have us a little fun."

Into a patch of devil's club I crawled. It was good cover, if I didn't scrape every inch of skin from my face. I crept forward. Easy. Quietly.

"Arr-oooooooh!" he howled, the call of a crazed wolf, echoing across the hillside.

I got to my feet and pushed through the alders to a stand of spruce. He might hear me, but he couldn't see me. It was too thick. It would buy me some time. Maybe I could slip out the other side. With enough cover—

"What I want to know," he shouted after me, "is why couldn't you just shoot the bear?"

What? I felt his beady eyes on me, taunting. Somewhere behind me. I stumbled, caught my footing and kept moving.

"You had me going for a while there. I admit. I was sure you were the real deal. But then you didn't shoot the bear."

He was moving. Which way now?

"That's when I saw you for who you really are."

I came to a halt. What did he mean? What was this all about?

"All your talk about being Little Miss Sharpshooter. Typical. Just like all the other women. All mouth. Running with the boys, just to be a tease. You think this is a game. A two week holiday from your otherwise boring life. You come out here for a little excitement. Act like a big hunter, but you're no hunter. You're a tease. You're all talk and you're only interested in boys with big guns. Like those brothers. They stroke their guns, pump up their egos, get off on pulling the trigger.

"But you didn't get to hunt with John-boy, did you. So you could bat your eyes and shake your little ass."

I dropped to a crouch. I had to get a bearing on him.

"They're not real men. They know nothing about being a man." He moved closer to me. "*I'm* a real man,"

Is that what this was about?

"Sure, Jack would have coddled you, helped you hold your gun, told you what a great hunter you are. But he wouldn't have brought in a bear like I did."

There was a long pause. I held my breath, sure he was listening for me to move.

"Mark, Jack, Bob—they don't know shit. I'm the best tracker. I'm the real hunter. You didn't know it, but I was the one you wanted. And I proved it. But you had to go and do what you did."

What? Not shoot the bear? Kiss Dalton? What?

"You don't deserve a real man," he said, his voice a growl. My hands started to shake again. Dalton was right. This wasn't about poaching. This guy was a madman.

"If you ain't the predator, you're the prey. It's a brutal world."

I shrank back, tucked into the pine boughs. He was only a few feet away. *Don't let him get to you. Stick to the plan, like you promised Dalton. Live and die by the plan. Get out of here.*

"What's it feel like being the one hunted?" I swear I heard him lick his lips. "You are feisty though. I was hoping for a feisty one."

Feisty is my middle name. He'd moved again. Closer. I ducked. Where was he?

"I bet you miss your daddy, don't you?"

The image of my father, my real father, flashed before me, hiding in the bushes, poachers surrounding him, moving in for the kill. *You leave my dad out of this.*

"He's not here to protect you, sweetheart. You're all mine to do with as I want."

I sucked in air. Rage churned in my belly. *You son of a bitch.*

"You're not going to disappoint me and give up without a fight, are you?"

Oh, I'll show you a fight. Adrenaline pumped through my veins.

"Oh, yes," he moaned. He was right behind me now, his voice husky. "I can smell your fear."

I'm not afraid of you.

"You're heart's thumping away in your chest. You're shaking. Why don't you run, little rabbit. Run!"

No more running.

"You're just a scared little girl."

I'll show you what this little girl can do.

CHAPTER 16

I dropped to my belly and wrapped my hand around a stick that was lying on the ground.

Every sense alert, I propped myself up on my elbows under the pine tree, waiting.

The subtle wisp of misty rain, accumulating on needles, then dripping to patter on the ground was the only thing I heard. Where was he? I turned my head to hear. Drip. Drop. Nothing.

The sound of my own breathing drowned out everything else. The beating of my heart thudded away—*thump thump, thump thump.*

I inched forward. Then I heard something. The snap of a twig. Which way? The whoosh of his pant leg against the brush. I kept hidden, scanning the forest floor. Then it was there, his boot. Five feet away.

He took another step. Then another, creeping toward me.

Just a few more steps. One, then another. His boot settled on the moss, two feet away. I drew back and thrust the stick into his calf. *Take that!* He reared backward. I grabbed his other foot and he toppled, landing flat on his back.

"You bitch!"

I sprang on top of him, my hands at his throat.

He bucked and shoved me, but I hung on. We rolled in the brush, slammed into a spruce. I closed my eyes as the branches scraped across my face.

Rocky's chuckle made me open them again. His hands were on my hips. "You wanna play do you?"

I drew back and slapped him across the face.

He laughed louder. Then his eyes narrowed. He shifted and flung me on my back, knocking the wind out of me. *Damn. How'd he do that?*

Then he was on top of me, pinning my arms back. I pivoted on my hip, shoved my arm out farther to break his balance. As he collapsed, I rammed my elbow hard against his throat. He fell over, hacking, surprise in his eyes.

I was on my knees and had one hand on the rifle when he swiped me with his left hand, right across the rash on my neck and hard on my ear.

"Ow!" I shrieked. I still had a hold of the rifle. It came free from his shoulder. I gripped it with both hands and struck him in the crotch with the stock.

On my feet, I ran, my arms pumping, my heart pounding, my lungs burning, my wounded leg moving faster than I thought possible. I barreled through thicket, plowed through bushes, up a ridge and down another, getting as far away as I could.

I couldn't beat him at hand-to-hand combat. He was well-trained, stronger. I was wounded, too. But now I had the rifle. I had the rifle! *Hallelujah! You're going down, you crazy son of a bitch!*

Ahead, there was a natural ledge. I climbed to the top, pushing my limits, then spun around to where I could see the path I had come before I stopped to catch my breath.

My lungs couldn't settle down. So I paced, puffing out the air, watching for him to chase, the rifle still in my hand.

I grabbed the bolt and racked it back. Empty. No bullets. *Dammit!* Of course he wouldn't carry it loaded, for this exact reason. It was for long distance. He had his sidearm, which was more securely fastened to his belt. *Dammit! What was I thinking? Why hadn't I grabbed that?*

Was there more ammo back in the box in camp? Dalton's and my guns were there. But would Rocky have left all the ammo there too once he left the camp? That's probably what he carried in the backpack. Or, if he was smart, he would have hidden it somewhere in the woods.

Dammit!

He'd be on my trail soon.

Settle down, McVie. The trap. Dalton will be there. Stick to the plan.

After a quick scan, I realized I'd run back in the direction where we'd hunted yesterday. Or was it two days now? Three? My hand went to my head, as if I could steady my thoughts. I needed food, water.

The rain had stopped, thankfully, though I was soaked through to my skin. The sun beat down from directly overhead, giving a hint of warmth. In the sky, further east, ravens circled with two vultures, their broad wings tipping on the wind. A sign of carrion below. Was I that close to the bear kill? If so, what other animals were gathered for the feast?

I didn't want to find out.

I needed to keep moving and lead him back around to the trap without running into any more trouble. If there were any animals feeding on the carcass or even in that blueberry patch that Dalton had found and— blueberries! The branches drooping with them, he had said.

Which way was it? That way. I pushed through the brush and there they were, bushes loaded with little, luscious spheres of blue. I dropped to my knees and grabbed at the branches, stripping them of handfuls of berries, and crammed them into my mouth. Oh so sweet! I didn't know blueberries could taste so good. I slumped to the ground and shoved berries into my mouth, eating as fast as I could pick them.

My brain signaled alarm bells. I had to be careful, move on.

Rocky couldn't be far behind. *Just one more handful.* Then back toward Dalton and the trap. Had it been enough time? Was he in place by now?

I got to my feet. From where I stood, I had two choices: head upward, through the open hillside, then drop back on the downward slope to the trap or head toward the lakeside now, push through the woods and the thick understory that lined the lake, then make my way back upward.

Either way had disadvantages and—whoosh! The ground at my feet exploded, spraying mud at my pant legs, and a split second later, the shot echoed inside my head.

I dropped to the ground, my full weight coming down on my injured thigh. I retched with pain. A patch of berry bushes burst into pieces beside me. I pushed and rolled as the second shot rang out. Then a third.

You're supposed to chase me! Not shoot at me!

Crawling on my hands and knees, I managed to get cover under a spruce. Wet branches let loose their droplets, soaking my head. Then I felt a burning sensation. In my arm. My coat sleeve had a rip in it, a hole. Blood oozed out. My left arm. *He shot me in my arm!*

With my right hand, I clenched my bicep, squeezing to suppress the blood flow. *Damn that hurts.* A few short breaths. *Shit.* I had to get to the trap. To Dalton.

What had I been thinking? Believing I could take on Rocky on my own. What have I done? I started to shake uncontrollably.

"You *are* a feisty one." Every one of my muscles tightened at the sound of his voice. Panic rumbled in my gut and threatened to spread. "More fun than I thought you were going to be."

Where is he? Which way?

"And looky there. Under the tree, like a Christmas present."

Shit! I rolled, got to my feet, and ran, my hand gripping my left arm, my head down.

Toward the trap. My foot caught. On a root. Something. I slammed to the ground, face down, knocking the wind out of me. I lay there, a quick moment to catch my breath, then got to my knees, to my feet, and I was running, fear carrying me forward.

I couldn't underestimate him again. He'd slept. Eaten. And he was bigger and stronger and more fit than I was. He could've caught me by now, if he hadn't been toying with me.

What if he was tired of that already? What if he decided to shoot at me again? Get it over with?

I needed cover. Downhill, into the forest that lined the lake. That was the way.

His laughter followed me—the wild, primal, blood-curdling shrieks of a hyena.

Chapter 17

Somehow I got to the woods. My leg on fire, my arm screaming with sharp jolts, the rash at my neck burning where the devil's club had done its work. But I'd made it. I'd made it this far. I gulped in air, trying not to think about how thirsty I was.

The forest here was white and black spruce, quaking aspen, and paper birch. Not the best cover, but better than being out in the open. I pushed forward. I had to get as much space between me and Rocky as I could. Without him losing my trail. He'd shown that wasn't likely.

I followed the shoreline, uphill from the water's edge, concentrating on putting one foot in front of the other. Wait—wasn't this where I'd encountered the moose? No, that was old growth. I had to get ahold of my dizziness, get focused.

"There you are, little rabbit."

I spun around.

Rocky stood thirty yards away, his crossbow trained on my chest.

My lungs seized, catching my breath in my throat.

"Thought you were getting away, did you?"

His eyes glowed with satisfaction in startling me.

There was thicket to my left, downed branches to my right, if I could—

"Don't even think about it. I'll shoot. Enough running."

He took a step closer to me. Then another. "Don't worry. I

wouldn't make a fatal shot. Just one to slow you down." He grinned, a wicked, sleazy grin that made bile stir at the back of my throat. "You're wearing me out. And we haven't even got to the fun part yet."

He took another step. "Don't get me wrong. I like the feisty ones. Full of spice." He opened his mouth slightly and his tongue flicked at me. "Maybe you'll buck like a pig in heat."

I shuddered, the taste of bile in my throat making my stomach flip-flop.

"Tell me you won't lie there like a dead fish." He cocked his head to the side, scrutinizing me, his reptilian eyes darting up and down my body. "No. You wouldn't. You've got too much fire in you. I knew I liked you. The moment you walked in the lodge, trying to hide your disgust for the place."

You knew? You saw right through me?

"Righteous little cowgirl princess." He closed the distance between us. "I'll take pleasure in taking you down off that pedestal." He jerked the crossbow downward. "Get on the ground."

I froze in place. No way was I getting on the ground.

He stomped toward me, grabbed me by my hair, and yanked my head down to his knees. "I said get on the ground, Bitch."

My knees collapsed and I was on my belly, my face in the moss.

"You better learn to listen. To obey. Do you hear me? No girl of mine defies me."

I nodded, trying to pacify him.

"That's better. Now look at me."

I turned my head, looked up at him, into those colorless eyes, eyes reflecting years of anger, pent up, twisted into a calculated rage. His hand rubbed at the bulge in his pants. "Oh yeah, that's it," he said with a grunt. "You're going to be my best yet. My finest trophy."

I fought back the nausea. If I showed any sign of revulsion, he'd kill me. I knew it, in my gut. He had to believe I felt beaten, that I'd given up.

He grabbed the back of my pants, and with an amazing strength, lifted me in the air and flipped me on my back. He dropped down on the ground between my legs, shoving them apart.

I shrank back, crawled with my elbows, trying to get away from him.

"Now, now," he said, grabbing my belt. "Enough playing hard to get." He set down the crossbow so he'd have both hands now, yet he still fumbled to get the buckle undone. I bit my lip, trying not to react. Not yet. "You'll do as I say." A pause. He cocked his head to the side. "Well now, we can't have that."

At first, I didn't know what he meant, but he took hold of my arm and examined the gunshot wound. With his other hand, he flipped off his pack, reached into it, and took out a first-aid kit. He ripped my coat open and without a word, doused my arm with hydrogen peroxide, then wrapped it with a bandage.

I kept still.

Once he taped it off, he leaned down. His lips to my ear, his hot breath on my neck, he said, "I want you alive and kicking." Slowly, he drew back, running his lips along my cheek. "Until I'm done with you."

Don't react. Wait for the right moment. Wait.

His hands squeezed my breasts.

Son of a bitch. "What are you waiting for?" I spat.

"Oh, now you want it, do you?"

I made myself look up at him, look into his eyes. Saw his dilated pupils. The sign of excitement. Of lust. Of reveling in his conquest.

"Tell me how you want it," he moaned.

I calmed my voice, my breathing. *This could work.* "Since I walked into that lodge and saw you across the room." I steeled myself. "I've been wanting you. I was hoping it would be out here. In the wild." I looked him in the eye. "Take off your pants."

There was hesitation in his look. Had I gone too far? Did he know what I was trying to do? Either way, he would lose. If he kept his pants on, he'd have a hard time doing what he wanted. If he pulled them down, he'd be vulnerable. *Go ahead. Pull down those pants.*

He reared back and slapped me across the face. The sting fueled my rage. I swung and clipped him in the jaw. He caught me by the wrist and slammed my arm back, pinning me to the ground. "I knew you'd be a scrapper," he said as he brought his knee up, ramming it into my thigh to keep me in place.

I screamed out in pain.

"That get you hot?" he growled.

The man was built like a tiger, all sinewy and quick, with the same dangerous unpredictability. But he'd underestimated me. I was counting on it.

"You gonna be a screamer, too?" He said it like that's what he wanted.

He fumbled at his belt with one hand, unsnapped his pants as he held me down with the other hand. "I'm going to give you something you'll never forget."

He underestimated me. I had one hand free. The moment his pants were lowered, I reached down, grabbed his balls, and yanked as hard as I could. Like starting a lawn mower, my self-defense instructor had said. *Pull!*

Rocky reared back, his face bright red, and let out a yowl like a speared pig. He fell back, right on top of the crossbow. *Dammit!*

I reached for his sidearm, but it was gone. Where? In his pack?

"You bitch!" he roared, his hands at his groin. "I'm going to kill you."

I rolled, got to my feet, and ran, one foot in front of the other, as fast as I could, my heartbeat thumping in my ears. Through the trees, up the hillside. Ignoring the throbbing pain in my leg, in my arm. My light head. I wasn't stopping until I got to the trap.

I could hear him behind me, crashing through the foliage, his footsteps thudding on the ground. *That's right. Follow me, you son of a bitch.*

My head down, I focused on nothing but speed. My chest heaved with my breath, lungs burning. I couldn't fall down. If I fell, he'd be on me again. Stay upright and run, run, run.

Behind me was a loud thump, then a curse. He must have fallen down. I kept running. Any distance I could gain, I needed.

I broke from the thick woods, ran up a ridge, my arms pumping, feeling nothing but adrenaline. The stream was ahead. Not far now. The stream. And the trap. And Dalton. He'd be there. He had to be there.

One stride. And another. And another.

There was the stream. Straight ahead.

Two more strides and my foot fell into place, right where I knew the trap to be. Another stride and I was past, running. Rocky right behind me.

What if he didn't step where I had? I slowed and turned. Rocky was there, almost at the edge of the creek, his eyes on me. He hesitated.

"What is it?" he said.

Run. Keep running.

Rocky looked down, around. "Why'd you hesitate? What is it about this place?"

Dammit. I dropped to my knees. "Just shoot me! Do it now. I'm tired of this!" I shouted.

A grin crept across his face. He raised his index finger and shook it at me like a father scolding a little child. "Oh no, little rabbit. You've been up to something. Haven't you?"

He raised the crossbow to put me in his sights and took a step toward me, his foot right on the trap. Or was it? Wasn't this the spot where we had hidden it? Nothing happened.

My heart stopped. Where was Dalton? Was he really dead? Shot back at the river? *Oh god! Dalton!*

Another step, and another. My body shook with anger and fear. Then Dalton reared up from the bushes and tackled Rocky, knocking him over. The crossbow flew out of his hands as the two tumbled into the bushes in a mass of grunts.

Dalton! Thank god! I scrambled toward them on my hands and knees, reaching for the crossbow. Dalton pummeled Rocky with his fists, but Rocky took it like he was jacked up on something. He didn't wince or pull away like a normal person would. It was as if he wanted it, welcomed it. When Dalton rose up, Rocky landed a punch in his kidney. Dalton doubled over.

"No!" escaped my lips. I grabbed hold of the crossbow.

Then they were wrestling again, arms and legs enmeshed, crashing through the brush. I couldn't make out one from the other. No way could I shoot.

Rocky was encumbered by the pack, but it didn't seem to slow him down. Rage was a powerful motivator. And Dalton was getting the brunt of it.

Then Rocky had a knife in his hand—or was it Dalton? No, it was Rocky. He sliced and red blood streamed down Dalton's arm. He jabbed again and Dalton slapped his hand away. Rocky flipped the knife in his hand and sliced back. Dalton blocked with his forearm but took a knee to the gut.

They were on the ground, rolling downhill again.

I pushed through the brush, keeping up.

Dalton broke free and kicked Rocky square in the jaw,

sending him backward, stumbling, trying to stay on his feet.

I raised the crossbow, tried to hold it steady to look through the scope, but Rocky had gained his balance and pounced on Dalton.

Dalton came up from the bushes with Rocky's sidearm in his hand, but Rocky lunged, sending it flying. Could I get to it? I had a weapon in my hands. A lethal weapon. A more accurate weapon. But a gun was a gun. I headed for it.

I pawed at the ground where the gun had fallen, scrambling through the bushes. *Where could it be?* I searched left, then right. *Dammit! Dammit all to hell!*

I popped my head up. The men were tumbling down the hill again. I took three strides before they came to a stop with a distinct moan. Dalton lay motionless, Rocky on top of him. I planted my feet and raised the crossbow, my whole body shaking.

"Get off of him!" I shouted.

Rocky's eyes slowly raised to focus on me.

"Get off of him right now!"

Slowly, measured, he rose, sitting atop Dalton, his chest facing me, fully exposed. Thirty yards away.

Holding the crossbow trained on his heart, I said, "It's over."

His eyes held mine, cold and hard. In an instant, he raised his knife and thrust it downward. Toward Dalton.

I pulled the trigger and let the arrow fly.

CHAPTER 18

Rocky fell backward, the arrow stuck in his chest, rage and shock in his eyes.

I raced down the hill toward Dalton as fast as my leg would take me.

The knife protruded from Dalton's thigh, his hand wrapped around it, his face white. Blood. There was too much blood.

I reached for the knife.

"No!" he grunted. "Don't take it out."

"What?"

His chest was heaving. "I'll bleed to death if—" he drew in air "—if you take it out." He panted to hold back the pain. "Make sure," he managed, nodding toward Rocky.

Rocky lay on the ground in a heap, his leg twitching. Dead. I'd killed him.

"I...I..." My stomach flipped. "I think I'm going to—" I leaned over and retched, vomit heaving from my stomach and onto the ground, the bitter, nasty taste of bile making me spit and gag.

"Breathe," Dalton was saying. "Stay with me. Just breathe."

I sat back, closed my eyes and drew in a long breath. Then released it, slowly, trying to find calm.

"I killed him." I puffed. "I shot a man."

"Poppy, focus. It's okay. Everything's going to be okay."

I nodded. My heart rate was slowing.

"Listen to me. You have to check. Make sure. Do you hear me?"

Nodding, knowing he was right, I stretched my reach as far as I could, not wanting to get any closer than I had to, and placed my index and forefinger on Rocky's neck. No pulse.

"He's dead," I said.

"Well it's about goddamn time," Dalton croaked and lay back.

"Yeah," I said, not knowing what else to say. I'd just killed a man. A man trying to kill me, trying to kill my partner, but still…I'd killed him. My stomach pulled tight, the acid bubbling back up.

"Take a breath," Dalton said.

I did.

"You look like hell."

My attention snapped back to him. "You don't look much better." Sweat beaded on his forehead. His hand that clutched the knife, holding it in place in his thigh, was white. "Let me take a look at that."

Blood oozed around the knife blade where it entered the skin, soaking his pants around it. "Do you think he hit your femoral artery?"

Dalton's lips were pursed into an O as he concentrated on his breathing.

"I'll take that as a yes. Okay." *Okay. Shit.* I stood to look. We were at least a quarter mile from the camp, maybe farther. "Okay," I said again.

I dropped to my knees next to Rocky, rolled him over onto his side, and ripped open his backpack.

All his daypack emergency gear was inside, but not the sat phone. *Damn.*

A tourniquet. That's what was needed.

I pulled a strap from the pack and quickly wrapped it around

Dalton's thigh, higher than the wound, and pulled it tight. An arrow was the best I had to cinch it. I tied one into the knot and twisted. Dalton winced.

"Too tight?"

He shook his head.

"Good." I tied the other end of the arrow just above his knee to keep the tension. "Here's what we're going to do. I'll run back to the camp and call for help. You—" I choked back my fear "—you stay alive. Okay?"

With gritted teeth, he nodded.

"I'll be right back, Dalton." I leaned forward and kissed him on the lips. "Don't you die on me, do you hear me? I'll be right back."

"Enough drama," he said, the muscles in his neck pulled tight. "Go already."

I got to my feet and ran. And ran. I had to get help. Now. A severed femoral artery was life threatening.

If Rocky had pulled the blade back out, Dalton would be— my hand went to my mouth. I couldn't say it. I couldn't think it.

Keep running. Keep running!

I came up over the ridge and saw the camp over the next rise. There I would get the phone, call in the calvary, then race back to keep him stable.

The gate was closed, the electric fence still energized. I gripped the plastic handles to unclip the wires as fast as I could, then moved right to the storage box. Our guns, boxes of food stuff—*food!* I shoved the crackers and bananas into a pack then continued sorting through the box, tossing the contents on the ground—cast iron skillet, box of matches, can of coffee, utensils, two blankets, camp chairs, the tent bags, a first-aid kit. No phone.

I spun around. "Dammit! Damn him to hell! Where's the phone?"

I raced to Rocky's tent. His sleeping bag and pillow got shaken, tossed out. Extra socks. Nothing else. Nothing.

What had he done with it?

The only place left in camp was our tent. I rummaged through it. Nothing there. As I'd thought, all the ammo was gone too. I scanned the hillside. Where would he have hidden it? There was no way of knowing. It might as well have been on the moon.

I grabbed the bag of food, a jug of water, a sleeping bag, and the first-aid kit and headed back to Dalton.

His eyes were closed but he was conscious when I got back.

"Do you want the good news or the bad news?" I asked, bent over, heaving to catch my breath.

His pupils looked a little dilated. Not good.

"Food," I said, holding up a rucksack. "How about a banana?"

He didn't make a sound or move.

"Okay, let's start with water," I said. I unscrewed the top of the jug and held it to his lips. "C'mon, just a sip."

He tried to drink, his hand tightening around the knife in his thigh.

As he lay his head back, his eyes met mine. "No phone?"

I shook my head. "And Joe won't be expecting us back for at least, well, a few more days, assuming—" I looked over at the body, at Rocky, lying there in a heap and my throat constricted—*don't think about that* "—he checked in, which I'm willing to bet he did."

He nodded and drew in a deep breath.

I pried open the first-aid kit. "I don't suppose there's a field technique for—" I stared at the knife sticking out of his thigh "—for that?"

He gave me a sideways grin. "Yeah. You order a body bag."

"No way. Not on my watch," I said. If the knife had to stay in, well, we'd make sure the knife stayed in.

I packed mounds of gauze around the blade, then used the entire roll of tape, round and round his thigh, to keep it in place.

"I'm getting you out of here." I risked a glance at Rocky's body one more time, lying there dead, and down at the plane, floating on the lake. "You watch me. Sit tight."

"What are you thinking?" Dalton managed.

"The plane. It can't be that hard to fly."

His eyes grew wide. "You can't be serious."

"You need a hospital. Now."

"Build three fires. Lots of smoke. Someone will see."

"Like who? We haven't seen another soul, not a plane, nothing, since we've been out here."

"Someone will come. Eventually. You have the supplies now. You'll be fine."

"But you won't."

He shook his head. "It's not worth the risk."

"Not worth the risk? Your life is not worth the risk? You listen to me, mister. You keep pressure on that leg. You stay awake. And you live. Do you hear me? We're taking that plane and getting the hell out of here."

His eyes focused on the plane. I could tell he was contemplating the distance, how he'd get to it.

"You leave that up to me," I said. "I'll get you there."

"Your arm," he said, noticing my bandage for the first time. "How'd you—"

"It was Rocky actually. Don't worry. Another flesh wound. Nothing serious."

In a stand of alders I found two downed limbs, long enough for what I needed. This had to work. He couldn't die on me now. It had to work. It would work.

With the two branches laid out parallel, I stretched the

sleeping bag between them. From Rocky's pack, I found some nylon cord. Using Dalton's jackknife, I cut holes in the sleeping bag at intervals where I could lace the cord, tying the bag to the branches.

I laid my makeshift travois next to Dalton. "Let's get you on here," I said. He was too exhausted to argue when I rolled him on his side, pulled it up under him, then rolled him onto it.

With a push of sheer determination, I took hold of the branches and lifted, and with one step, then another, I dragged him down the hillside.

CHAPTER 19

At the edge of the lake, I dropped to the ground, exhausted.

The sun was behind the trees. It had to be at least three o'clock.

Dalton must have been reading my mind. "It's too late. Even if you do get that thing running, and up in the air without killing us, it will be dark. Trying to land in the dark is suicide."

I stood up and shoved my coat off, then my shirt and pants. "I'm getting that plane," I said. "I'm getting you in it. Then we'll see."

"That water's ice cold. You're already exhausted."

"It'll revive me," I said. "Stop arguing."

He closed his eyes, resigned.

"You just sit tight," I said and waded in.

It's amazing how quickly legs can go numb. By the time I plunged full in, my breath came in short pants and my muscles threatened to seize. But I had to get there. To the plane. Back to Dalton.

I kicked and threw my arms forward, pushing through the icy water. One stroke. Then another. Then another. And I was there, pulling myself up onto the pontoon. I half-expected the door to be locked but it flung open when I grabbed the handle. I crawled inside and went straight for the radio. Dalton had said it was disabled, but I had to check. The knob turned, but nothing happened. Was there a wire I could reattach?

Something?

Forget it. Dalton would have checked all that. I went for the flight manual in the side pocket.

How to start the engine. It had to be in the first pages. I flipped page after page, shivering. Drawings. Specs. Lists of equipment. *Oh crap.* Maybe this was just a maintenance manual? No. There. `Start Engine.`

`Battery master switch - ON.` I peered at the dash, all buttons and switches, knobs and levers. *Crap. C'mon!*

I flipped back through the pages to the diagram of the dashboard, ripped it from the book, then opened back to the page on how to start the engine.

`Battery switch.` Okay, got it.

`Fuel selector to fullest tank.` Got it.

`Mixture lever - AUTO RICH.` What did that mean? There was no setting for auto rich. I pushed the mixture lever forward, half way. Would that do it?

My hands shook, my teeth chattering. "Can we get some heat in here!" I shouted to no one. *Where's the damn purser when you need her?*

I could do this. I had to do this.

`Throttle lever - 1/4 to 1/2 in. OPEN.` Ok, got it.

`Build up pressure with wobble pump to maximum 5 psi.` *Wobble pump? Seriously? There really is a wobble pump?*

Right there on the page. Wobble pump. Fuel pressure. The lever was in the center, between the seats. I gave it a few pumps up and down. It made a whoosh, whoosh noise. Definitely gas in the lines.

`Prime 4 strokes.` *Prime what? How?*

I scanned the dash schematic. Nothing. Was there an index in this thing? I flipped to the back. No index. A shiver took over and I shook uncontrollably, rubbing my arms. I bounced in the chair. Get that blood flowing.

What was I thinking? I don't know how to fly a plane. *I'm going to get us killed.*

No. *You can do this. You have to do this.*

Back over the schematic again. It had to be there. My finger shook as I dragged it across the sheet, checking each word. There. Primer. *There it is!* On my left side, a small knob next to the seat. I worked it up and down until it got harder to push. *That must be enough.*

`Both ignition switches to ON position.` Switched on.

`Hold starter switch to STARTER position.` Okay.

The starter whined, but the engine didn't turn over.

`Hold Booster Coil switch to BOOSTER COIL position. As soon as engine fires, release the switch.`

"Here goes," I said aloud and held the switch. With a rattle, the engine fired to life. The propeller started turning. I let out a whoop.

Quick. Off with the starter and booster coil switches.

The plane rattled and shook as the engine huffed and sputtered, then quit.

"Dammit!"

What? More throttle? More priming? More wobble? Wobble. *Oh my god. It comes down to a wobble.* I giggled. Then I laughed. My eyes started to well up with tears. *No! Dammit! We are not going to die out here!*

"Listen to me, bitch!" I slammed my fist on the dash. "You're going to fly. You're going to fly me back to that lodge. Do you hear me? Me and Dalton. Right now."

I shoved the throttle lever forward, then back. Cranked on the wobble pump a few more times, then flipped the starter switch on. She whined, the starter turning. I pushed the booster coil switch again. She shook and sputtered to life. Up with the throttle. "Don't you quit on me!"

She reached a steady hum. *Yes!*

Okay. Now to get her in motion. Next page. Next page. There.

`Taxiing.`

`Flaps at CRUISE POSITION.` What's cruise position? Does it really matter? I'd fiddle with them once I got her moving.

`Propeller lever - full INCREASE rpm.` Got it. I pushed the lever and the engine got louder and the plane started to move. Excellent.

`Watch oil and cylinder temps.` Ah, sure.

`Operate rudder pedals to steer airplane by means of steerable tailwheel.` I placed my feet square on the pedals and pushed one, then the other. Okay, got it.

The plane jerked to a halt. *Crap. The anchor.*

I pulled back on the propeller lever, flung the door open and jumped out onto the pontoon. How was I going to pull up an anchor? Wait. I wouldn't need it again. I untied the line and let it go.

Back in the cockpit, I shoved the propeller lever forward, moved the foot pedals back and forth, and got her pointed toward shore. Toward Dalton.

"Wake up." I slapped him across the face. "C'mon. Wake up."

Dalton's eyes fluttered.

"Wake up, damn you!"

One eye opened.

"C'mon. I got the plane. Get in."

I'd managed to get the plane turned and stopped in about two feet of water, rather than bring her nose right up on the beach. I wasn't sure if there was a reverse and didn't want to risk getting stuck now.

The plane was floating without any tether, the propeller slowly turning.

"C'mon. Now." *Before she floats away.* "Get on your feet, soldier."

With a shove, I got him sitting upright. He saw the plane then. His eyes narrowed then flicked toward me.

"All you have to do is get in the passenger seat. I'll do the rest."

With a groan, he shifted his weight to his good leg and slowly pushed himself upward.

"I'm right beside you, holding you steady."

He raised himself to his full height and focused on the plane. "Just my luck," he mumbled. When he put his weight on his bad leg, the pain must have been unbearable, but he didn't show it. SEALs.

I got up under his arm. "Lean on me," I said.

He didn't slow. Into the water and up onto the pontoon he hobbled. With those strong arms, he pulled himself into the cockpit and swung into the seat, panting to abate the pain. It had taken all he had.

In the pilot's seat again, I thrust the throttle lever forward, worked the foot pedals, and pointed her toward the middle of the lake. The sky was clear, but the clock was ticking.

"McVie."

"What?" I turned. "Did you say something?"

I reached over him, grabbed his earphones from the hook and snapped them over his ears, adjusting the mic.

His voice raspy, he said, "Have I ever told you—" he drew in a needed breath "—you're incorrigible?"

"Yeah, I think so," I said with a smile.

"Well, in case—" A cough. "—in case we don't—"

"We're going to make it, Dalton. I can do this."

He nodded, his eyes closed. "I know. I just—" His eyes

fluttered back open. "I just want you to know—" Those eyes held mine. "Thank you, partner." And he was out again.

I reached over his chest, pulled the seatbelt down and clipped it into place. Then I put mine on too.

Holding the manual in my hand, I flipped to the page titled, "Take Off."

All levers in place.

`Flaps - TAKE-OFF position.` What position is that? I shuffled through a few more pages to the diagram. Okay, got it.

Face into the wind. The manual didn't state that, but I knew it. And I needed lots of lake.

`Mixture at full rich.`

`Open throttle smoothly to maximum permissible take-off power. See figure 4-1.` Figure 4-1 showed the gauges. Green good. Yellow caution. Red danger. Simple enough. *Maximum it is.*

`Allow aircraft to fly itself off at 55 to 65 mph in a tail down attitude and climb at 65 mph.` *Tail down attitude?* Did that mean nose up? We were going to find out.

Easy now. The voice of my father in my head. Nothing drastic. *Easy touch.*

Deep breath.

"Hang on," I said to Dalton as I grabbed hold of the throttle lever and shoved it all the way forward.

The propeller started spinning faster and faster, the hum rising in volume as the plane moved through the water, building speed.

We were doing this thing.

The mph gauge needle rose, up, up. 45mph. Then 50. 55. 57. 60. We were still on the water, the pontoons slapping in the waves. Then it happened. We were airborne. But the plane veered drastically to the left. I shoved the rudder right and she corrected, still climbing, leaving my stomach on the lake.

I took hold of Dalton's hand and squeezed. "We're going to make it. Stay with me now. We're going to make it."

The plane climbed, smooth as can be, like I'd been flying one for years.

`Slowly increase airspeed to 80 mph and re-trim.` Throttle forward.

"We're flying!"

Once we got to 500 feet, the manual said to set flaps to climb. Did I want to continue to climb? This seemed high enough for me. The higher we flew, the more we'd have to descend. I quickly read through the section on climbing and cruising. Nowhere did it say what altitude to fly. 500 feet felt right to me. I set the flaps to cruise position and the plane leveled. Good.

The flight out to the camp had been about forty-five minutes on a south-southeast path. Using the rudder, I turned to head north-northwest. Back to the lodge. Trying to fly all the way to Anchorage wasn't an option. We'd have to take our chances that Joe hadn't been compromised.

Getting a feel for the flaps, the rudder, the trim, was a priority. They'd be needed for landing. Back to the manual, I read through the section on landing.

Caution. Notes. Fuel tank capacity. Airspeed correction.

Finally, a section titled "Descent." There were three lines:

`Reduce airspeed and power as required.`
`Fuel selector to fullest tank.`
`Instruments in correct ranges.`

What? That's it? What's required? What are the correct ranges? I looked at Dalton, passed out in the passenger seat. *Oh shit.*

Under "Landing," the same. `Trim as required.`

There were sections on cross-wind landing and minimum run landing. Then the post flight checklist.

What have I done?

We were flying. Committed. But flying was one thing. Landing was something else. This plane was coming down eventually. One way or another.

Okay. Don't freak out!

Landing was just a controlled descent, right? Slowly, take her down, until the pontoons touch the water. Easy. The lodge was on a river, so I had all the distance I needed. That was a plus.

First, I had to find the lodge.

I reached over and placed my fingers on Dalton's neck to check his pulse. Slow, but there.

Blue sky spread before me. Green and yellow hills below. A beautiful landscape. Would it be the last I'd see?

Stop thinking like that.

My mom. Would I see her again? And Chris. I had to call him. First thing and plan that trip to Mexico like he wanted. What if I didn't—*McVie. Cut it out.*

I checked the clock. Only fifteen minutes in the air. Thirty to go. *If* I had the right heading. I should be able to see the river though. Then follow it until I spotted the lodge. Then circle back for landing. That's what I'd do. That was the plan.

Double checking the manual for landing tips seemed like a prudent thing to do, so I scanned the table of contents. Description of the aircraft. Procedures. Operating limits. Special installations. Data charts.

Nothing helpful.

Info on the propeller, the rudder, trim, flaps. All there. But what to do with that information? What angle was right? What trim?

I took hold of the yoke, my feet on the pedals, and slowly made adjustments, easy now, feeling the plane dip and turn. That was my best option. Feel it.

Dalton moaned. Sweat beaded on his forehead. I took his hand in mine. He'd risked his life for me. And it wasn't the first time. Now, were we going to die together? Without me telling him how much I—his eyes opened.

"Are we there yet?" he said.

"Almost. Make sure your tray table is in the upright position," I said, trying to manage a smile.

The way he looked at me made my stomach flutter. Then it clenched with dread. "I'm sorry I got you in to this."

He closed his eyes. "Don't be sorry." He opened them again. "We're in this together."

My stomach fluttered again and I turned so he wouldn't see the tears in my eyes. Deep breath. I turned back. "I'm going to land this plane."

"I know you will." His eyes winked shut.

"I mean it," I said, squeezing his hand, making him open his eyes and look at me. "I'm going to land this plane and get you to a hospital. I swear it."

"I know, Poppy. I know." And his eyes closed again.

I let go of his hand and gripped the yoke. *I will land this plane.*

The landscape stretched before me, a blur of fall colors. There, ahead. The river. It had to be the one.

I sat up straight. This was it. The plane seemed to putt along, taking its sweet time. Finally, the river was nearly below us. I turned the plane, easy now, to follow. The lodge had to be here somewhere. A mile. Another mile.

There it is! That's it. That's the lodge. That big old eye sore. Was I glad to see it, standing out like a beacon.

I went past, then turned the plane in a big, easy circle and lined up with the river. Throttle back. The engine hum slowed. Flaps set to landing. Throttle back some more. Slow. Dropping.

My hands gripped the yoke. We were coming down. Was it too fast? Throttle back some more. Glide in. That's the way. The trees got bigger. Closer. Dropping.

"Keep the nose up."

"What?" I turned.

Dalton's expression was adamant. "Keep the nose up!"

"Right."

I pulled back—easy—on the yoke. We were level with the treetops. Throttle back. Easy now.

Dropping fast. Maybe more throttle? *Shit!*

The pontoons slapped hard on the water, whipping my head forward.

We bounced up, the nose pointing to the sky, slamming me back in my seat. Then dropped flat, the floats crashing into the water, pitching us forward. I yanked the yoke back, but it was too late. The nose dove. The propeller rammed into the shallow water and hit bottom, breaking off with a bang as we rolled. Glass shattering. Metal crumpling. Over and back up again, everything spinning. Then the plane tipped backward and the tail hit the water with a sploosh.

Then all was still. Quiet. I let out my breath.

Dalton stared at me with that half-grin. I burst out laughing.

Chapter 20

We sat in the cockpit, staring at each other, my heart thrumming in my ears, my hands shaking.

Dalton gazed out the broken window, a contented smile on his face.

"You seem awfully calm," I said.

"I knew…" His voice shook, strained. "I knew you…could do it."

The whir of an outboard engine grew louder. The pontoon boat coming closer.

I unclipped my seatbelt, took my headphones off, then Dalton's before pushing the door open and stepping out onto the plane's float, which was bent at an awkward angle.

I had to be cautious. If Rocky had called and given us up…

Irene was at the helm, some man beside her. The other guide? I couldn't remember his name.

"Are you all right?" she shouted as they approached.

I shook my head, pointing to the passenger side. "Dalton! He's hurt!" They pulled up alongside. "He needs a hospital, right away."

The other guide—Jack, that was his name—stepped off the boat, onto the plane float, opened the door on Dalton's side, and peered in at Dalton. His eyes came to a halt on Dalton's leg and the knife sticking out of it. "What the hell happened?"

he asked, alarm clear on his face.

"Help me get him out," I said, crawling over the pilot's seat. "Don't move the knife."

His lips pursed in a sympathetic owe, he didn't hesitate. He took Dalton by the arm. "You awake, buddy? Can you move?"

Dalton nodded, a subtle, but determined nod.

Irene had the boat tied off and got on the other side of Jack. One under each arm, they heaved Dalton up and onto the pontoon boat where he slumped onto the bench chair.

I followed, sliding onto the chair next to him. "Go, go, go!" I hollered.

Irene obeyed, understanding the severity of the wound, the importance of expediency. There'd be time for explanations later. The boat engine fired to life and she was on the radio, shouting orders to someone.

Jack knelt in front of Dalton, a first-aid kit in his hands.

"How long has it been? Has he lost a lot of blood?" he asked as he stuck a needle in Dalton's arm, then donned surgical gloves and started poking at the gauze I'd packed around the knife.

"A couple hours?" I said. "We were up on a hill. It took some time to get him down to the water, to the plane."

He nodded, taking in the information, but the expression on his face was grim.

"Do you think—" I couldn't say it. "Is he going to—"

He gave me an encouraging smile.

"Thank God we've got two planes," Irene said, setting down the radio. "Jack'll fly him straight to Anchorage."

My head was buried in Dalton's chest, holding him upright, holding him close. All I could do was nod. It was out of my hands now. If Dalton was going to live, it depended on others. On time. On the weather. On the—*oh god*. I sat upright. "Can you fly at night?"

Jack nodded. "We'll get him there."

When the pontoons hit gravel, I looked up. Joe stood on shore. In two strides he was onboard and had me in his arms. "Oh my sweet daughter, what's happened?" His eyes landed on Dalton and the knife in his leg, then back to me, full of questions. "What happened?" He looked lost, wanting to help, but Jack was there, tending to Dalton.

"Oh Daddy, it was awful." I collapsed into his embrace, his arms, as if he really were my dad, my real dad. Thankful he was alive. The op hadn't been compromised. And Dalton was going to be all right. He had to be.

The brothers appeared with a stretcher, easing Dalton down onto it.

I tried to help but the ground moved, the world spun. Joe was there, holding me upright. "Take it easy," he was saying. "We've got him. You take it easy now."

"But—"

"But nothing. Sit back down. Daddy's here now." He hugged me tight and stroked my hair. And I remembered. I was Poppy Pratt, spoiled daughter of a rich oil tycoon. In her Daddy's arms. I let the tears flow. "Don't let him die."

"Everything's going to be okay," he soothed, rocking me. "Daddy's here."

"I got Mark on the radio. He's in the air, headed straight here," Irene said. "Maybe twenty minutes."

"Twenty minutes!" I sat upright. "That's too long."

Jack patted me on the knee. "It's all right. You kept the knife in. That was smart."

I managed a nod. "But he's lost a lot of blood."

"Irene, did you call Anchorage? A medevac?" Jack asked.

"Too far out," she said, shaking her head. "We have to wait."

Jack tugged at the bandage on my leg, peeled it back. My thigh had turned purple and yellow and the wound site oozed some nasty stuff. "I'll take him to the hospital then turn right around and come back for you."

Dalton was white, passed out, but Jack stayed with him, keeping a close eye on the wound. I sat next to him on the gravel shore. Waiting.

"It's too long. It's been too long. Too much blood lost," I said. I'd failed. He was going to die.

"We're not giving up yet," Joe said.

Finally, the plane came into view, the steady hum of the prop like the sound of salvation. It pulled up on shore, the propeller left slowly spinning as the brothers joined Mark, helping him to remove the back seat, then the passenger seat. They dropped them on the gravel shore, then hurried to carry Dalton on the stretcher toward the plane.

I yanked out of Joe's embrace. "I've got to go with him."

"There's no room," Mark said. "Jack will be with him."

"But—"

"It's in God's hands now," Mark said. "You have to let him go."

I stared. Frozen. *In God's hands?* This, from a poacher. I wanted to scratch his eyes out. Rip his heart from his chest. Scream, *this is all your fault* as I bashed his skull against the gravel. Instead, I leaned into Joe's arms and watched the plane taxi down the river, then lift off into the darkening night.

Irene fussed with my leg wound, dousing it with alcohol. "We don't want that to get infected," she said, making a painful face as I winced. "This will have to do until Jack gets back for you."

They'd brought me inside, into the great room, with all the dead animal heads hanging on the walls. And the fireplace. Oh the warmth. I wasn't sure I'd ever be warm again.

Irene pressed some gauze to my leg wound and secured it

with tape as her eyes traveled to the wound on my arm. "You look like you've been to war."

I nodded, thankful for her kindness.

Mark sat down across from me. "What the hell happened out there?"

I glanced at Joe.

"You know what," he said, "let's just give her some space. She's had a shock."

Townsend frowned but got up from the chair. "I'll make some tea."

Joe nodded a thanks and took my hand, but Irene didn't budge.

"I knew it," she muttered. "I knew that Rocky was trouble."

"What did you say?" Joe asked.

"Nothing," she said with a sigh. She shook her head, her gaze shifting to the rash at my neck. "I've got some salve for that." She rose and left to go get it.

"Just relax," Joe said. "We've got nothing but time. We'll get this all sorted out later. Lay your head back and relax."

"I can't. Where's the plane? I have to get to Dalton, he—"

"Don't you worry about Dalton right now. Just try to relax. Close your eyes."

"No. I can't. I have to know about Dalton."

"I promise. You'll be the first to know. Trust me. Just close your eyes."

I lay back, every muscle complaining. *Maybe just close my eyes for a bit.*

Someone grabbed my arm. I sat upright with a jolt, my heart racing. "What?" Where am I? It was warm. My head heavy, groggy. Were we—"Dalton?"

"He's stable," Joe said, letting go of my arm and sitting

down next to me. "They got to the hospital in time. Jack is already headed back here to pick you up."

Relief rushed over me and I felt like I might collapse. My eyes turned misty. He was going to be all right. I drew in a long breath, tried to relax.

Townsend was sitting on the chair across from me, Irene beside him. Both wore expressions of concern.

"Are you ready to tell us what happened?" Mark asked.

I glanced at Joe. He nodded. "Tell us everything."

"Well," I said, hesitating. Everything? *Crap*. Dalton and I hadn't talked about our story. It didn't matter. The kiss—the kiss wasn't relevant. Unless Rocky had called. I looked at Mark, trying to read him. "I'm not sure, to be honest. We flew out to the spike camp. Got set up. Everything seemed fine. I guess. The next day, Rocky took us to look for the bear. He spent all day but didn't find it and he was upset about that."

Mark nodded. That made sense to him.

"He was more than upset. He was…distraught?"

"How do you mean?"

"Like he was embarrassed maybe? Anyway, the next day—" *Rocky shot the bear?* No, no need to mention that. "He found the bear, but I missed the shot. Well, after we got back to camp, Rocky said he forgot the phone in the plane and took off to get it." I paused. "We assumed he was going to call you. Did he call?" I watched his response.

"No," Mark answered. Innocently. "Not a peep since you headed out to the spike camp, not until Irene called me to come back with the plane."

I looked to Joe for confirmation. He gave me a subtle shake of his head. If Rocky called, he wasn't aware of it.

"When he got back to camp, he pulled a gun on us and started shooting. For no reason."

All three shared the same look of surprise and confusion.

"Dalton and I took off running. For the next two days,

he—" I closed my eyes. *Stay true to character.* "Daddy, it was awful. He had his crossbow and he—" I swallowed hard "—he hunted us."

"What!" Joe looked truly shocked. He couldn't be sure if I was telling the truth or making it all up to maintain my cover. Either way, he played along. "You're saying he, he—"

"He chased me and shot at me. He shot Dalton too, but..."

"I knew something like this would happen," Irene muttered, holding her head in her hands.

Mark shut her up with a glance.

I looked to Joe. "He was crazy. Like he went wild."

Joe turned to Mark. "What the hell kind of psycho did you have working for you?"

Mark held his hands up in defense. "I had no idea. Honest. I'm as shocked as you are. I mean, Rocky was a bit odd, but—"

"A bit odd?" Joe rose to his full height. "He shot at my daughter and stabbed my son! You sent my children out into the wilderness with this man, knowing he was psycho?" He had his chest puffed out in full papa bear mode. "What the hell kind of operation are you running here?"

Mark stood toe to toe with Joe. "I'll get to the bottom of this," he said, his jaw set with determination. He turned to me. "Where is he now? Still at the spike camp then?"

"He's—" My eyes went from Mark to Joe then back. "He's dead." A flicker of surprise showed in Joe's eyes. "He and Dalton got in a fight. The knife, he—" I left it at that. Too many details wouldn't be prudent right now.

"Why didn't you call for help?" Joe asked.

"We couldn't find the phone. I think he hid it somewhere. The radio in the plane was disabled. I tried to fix it, but...I had to get Dalton to a hospital. I had to—" Tears welled up in my eyes again.

Mark glared at me in disbelief. "So you thought it was a good idea to try to fly a plane?"

"That's enough." Joe sat back down and wrapped his arms around me. "She's been through enough. The damage to your plane is inconsequential."

"Inconsequential?" He shifted on his heels. "This is my livelihood."

Irene held out a hand to Mark. "I don't think—"

"How dare you?" Joe rose back up from the chair and faced him down, his eyes enraged with fire. "I'm going to sue your ass from here to the South Pole and back. As soon as I get to Anchorage and get my lawyers on the phone, I'll—"

Mark's hands shot up in defense, his expression quickly changing from anger to realization, then to a placating smile. Lawyers meant investigations. "Let's not get carried away. I see your point, of course. I'm sorry. I wasn't thinking. This has all happened so fast." He sat back down. "You're right. The important thing is you got your brother back here," he said to me. "You were very brave."

I nodded, accepting his apology, but Joe wasn't having any of it.

"That's enough. Now leave my daughter be. She needs rest."

Mark's gaze dropped to his hands and he nodded. Irene took him by the arm and led him out of the room, shutting the door behind them.

Joe's eyes followed them out, then turned to me. In a whisper, he said, "Is that what happened?"

I nodded.

"Was your cover blown?"

"No, we don't think so. That's the thing, he—" And the tears surged to my eyes.

"Jesus," he said, shaking his head. "I'm sorry."

"Oh my god. Oh my god. I killed him, Joe. I killed him."

He sat down next to me and took me in his arms.

"He stabbed Dalton and I did it. I shot him with the bow."

Sobs wracked my body and I shook.

Joe rocked me, stroking my hair. "It's all right," he kept saying. "It's all right. You did what you had to do."

Snot ran from my nose and stuck in my hair. Joe reached for a tissue box on the table and handed it to me.

"He chased me, hunted me, like a..." I couldn't bring myself to say it. "And then the trap, it didn't work maybe? Or maybe Dalton was worried because he was holding the bow? I don't know."

"The trap? What trap?"

"Well, there was this bear trap and Dalton, he didn't—"

"You know what. That doesn't matter right now. Listen to me," he said. "You defended your partner. You risked your own life to save his getting him back here. You're a hero."

I shook my head and more tears gushed from my eyes.

"We're officers of the law. We put ourselves in harm's way. We never know what that might mean. He was a very bad man. You defended yourself and Dalton." He wiped a tear from my cheek. "You did your job."

I snuffled, trying to get myself together. "What's going to happen? I mean, here? What about—"

"You let me worry about that," he said and pulled me back into his bear hug embrace.

CHAPTER 21

Next to his bed, bags of blood and saline hung from hooks, plastic tubes running down into his arm. The sounds of beeps and clicks, his steady breathing helped by a machine, the potent scent of disinfectant—all reminded me of being in this same position in Costa Rica.

Maybe I was a bad partner. Last time he got shot. Because of me. This time stabbed. Maybe I deserved to be investigated. Maybe I was brazen and…maybe I wasn't cut out to be an agent. Dalton deserved a better partner.

He lay there, asleep. My heart ached for him to wake, to tell me he was all right, to show me that half-grin, one more time.

I sat down on the edge of Dalton's bed, took his hand in mine. "You're gonna be all right," I said, wishing he could hear me. "For a while there, I wasn't sure, but they say—"

The nurse came in. "We're doing everything we can," she said, checking the knobs and fiddling with the tubes and wires in the machine next to him. "You're not supposed to be out of bed. You need to rest yourself, young lady. " She gave me a motherly look, hands on her hips. "Let me help you back to your room."

"No. I've been sleeping too much."

"Oh my."

I spun around. Chris stood in the doorway. I sprang to my

feet and into his arms. "You got my message!"

"I was in Chicago and hopped a flight right away."

"Oh Chris, I'm sorry. I'm so sorry."

"What are you prattling on about?" He led me back to the chair. "Sit down. Take a breath."

The nurse smiled at us as she left the room.

"Your job. My big mouth. Chris, I can't believe I was so stupid. I don't know what I was thinking."

He grinned. "You never could hold that tongue."

I shook my head, filled with relief. "I promise, I'll—"

"All right. All right. Enough already. I forgive you."

I hugged him again, holding on tight, needing to feel his strength.

When he eased back from my embrace, he looked me up and down. "What the hell happened, girl? You look like shit."

"Yeah, well."

He turned toward Dalton, concerned.

My eyes got misty. "Every time I come in here to see him, he's sleeping."

Chris pulled me close with one arm, squeezing me to him. "What do the doctors say?"

"He lost a lot of blood, but they say he's going to be fine."

"Well, then. I'm sure he will." His eyebrows shot up and with his teasing voice, he said, "The most important question then is: did you get the bad guy?"

My eyes dropped to the floor. I couldn't talk about it. Not yet.

Chris nodded in understanding. He saw the bandages on my arm and frowned. "I don't suppose it would do any good to try to convince you to take a desk job?"

I shook my head, smiled. Then giggles bubbled up from inside and we both burst into laughter. It felt good.

"You are taking a vacation with me though," he said, feigning a stern father's voice. "I won't take no for an answer."

I raised my right hand. "I promise." No argument from me. I needed a break. Some time to think. Some time with my best friend, to talk and—"Oh Chris. You had something you wanted to tell me. What was it? Tell me. Tell me please."

He shook his head. "Right now isn't—it can wait. You come on vacation with me and I'll tell you all about it. Deal?"

I nodded. "Deal."

"Hey there. Welcome back," Chris said, his eyes focused over my shoulder.

I spun around.

Dalton's face was still pale, but his eyes were lit with vigor. Relief came upon me like the warm sun breaking from behind a dark cloud.

"You're awake!"

His eyes held mine. My teeth clenched together and my lip quivered. I wanted to hug him, hold him, tell him how scared I'd been.

Chris put his hand on my arm. "I'm going to go. I'll be at the hotel."

I gave him a hug and a kiss on the cheek.

Once he'd left, I wrapped my arms around Dalton's neck and squeezed him tight to be sure he was really alive. "You're here. You're really okay."

"Thanks to you."

I sat back and stared at him, holding his hand in mine. There were so many emotions swirling around in my head. But Dalton was alive. That's all that mattered right now. Tomorrow I could worry about the rest.

He gave me a smile. "I've been thinking," he said. "We should—"

"I'm sorry. I shouldn't have kissed you. It was—"

"What?" His eyes softened. His eyes traveled to my lips and held there. "I'm quite sure that *I* kissed *you*."

My breath caught in my throat.

He squeezed my hand.

I exhaled. "We should what?"

"What?"

"You started to say, we should…"

"You know. When I get out of here, we should go out and do something. Together."

I couldn't help but grin. "Are you asking me out on a date?"

He held my gaze. "Would you say yes?"

"I might as well." I shrugged. "I mean, since I'll be fired and we won't be working together anymore."

He stared at me for the longest time, that mind of his weighing something.

"Nice to see you're up and well."

I swung around toward the door and the source of the voice. A man. I blinked. Stan Martin? "Omigosh, sir." I yanked my hand from Dalton's and started to get up, but he held out a hand, gesturing for me to stay seated. "What are you doing here? I mean, all this way and—"

"Two of my agents have been injured on duty. I wanted to come myself, make sure you're taken care of." He yanked the chair out from against the wall, sat down, smoothed his tie against his shirt, then looked up at me. "I take it you're feeling better."

It all came rushing back. The investigative hearing. My job on the line. And now I was going to have to explain shooting Rocky. "I know you have concerns—"

He held up his hand. "Don't worry about that right now." He gave me a warm, genuine smile. "I understand that if you hadn't taken the action you did, Dalton wouldn't be alive today."

"No. He's the one who saved me. He—"

The hand again. "I'm glad to see you humble. But Joe's already told me the whole story." His eyes went to Dalton and mine followed. "In fact, he's been singing your praises. From the sounds of it, you're a candidate for a medal of honor."

I turned back to Mr. Martin, keeping it together. "I'm sure that's not—"

"Poppy," Dalton interrupted. "You saved my life. The doc said if you hadn't got me back to the lodge when you did, I would have bled out for sure. I wouldn't have made it through the night."

My stomach clenched. This was too—*get a grip*. I pasted on a cordial smile and said to Mr. Martin, "I can't believe you came all the way to Alaska."

"Actually, I wanted to talk to you two anyway. Give you the news in person."

I shot a glance at Dalton. What news? Dalton shrugged.

"The President has created a task force, an elite team, if you will," Martin said, "to investigate animal-related cases. Wildlife and domestic." He hesitated, as though what he was about to say he wasn't sure he wanted to share. "You're participation was specifically requested. In fact," he cleared his throat, " it was more like a demand."

He was looking at me. "Me?"

"You are the one who single-handedly apprehended Ray Goldman, our most-wanted, are you not?" His face looked like he was actually in physical pain as he spit out those words. Either that or constipated.

"Yes. I mean, Dalton and I did. Together. We're a team."

"Indeed. And I'm glad to hear you say that."

"Did you say the President, sir? Of the United States?"

"Yes, *the* President of the United States."

I turned to Dalton. He was grinning. "Your mouth is hanging open."

I snapped it shut.

"I reported that you two need some time to recuperate. As soon as you're up to it, you'll join the team. That is, if you want to?"

I nodded, then caught my head bobbing. An elite task force. I couldn't believe it.

"But sir," I said. "This op, there was an incident and—"

"Yes," he said with an exaggerated nod. "Joe told me about that. A hunting accident. Unfortunate, but, it happens." He straightened his tie. "We did a little digging. It seems the man in question was wanted in Iowa for assault, kidnapping, and multiple weapons offenses. I guess they can close the case."

Was that it? I'd killed a man and it would be scribbled in a report, stuck in a manila folder in the back of a file cabinet somewhere, as a hunting accident? Was that justice?

"What about Townsend?" I asked.

"Joe will be by later this evening to fill you in."

"Okay, but Irene, his wife, doesn't know about the poaching. I'm sure of it," I said. "She shouldn't be arrested."

"Put it in the report," Martin said, nodding in understanding. "But I don't believe Joe plans to arrest anyone just yet. The man's got a dead body on his hands. We'll see how he deals with that." He gave us an amused smirk. "Joe seems to really be enjoying making Townsend squirm. This Rocky fellow might have acted on his own trafficking in wildlife parts, but Joe's convinced Townsend was complicit in the poaching. The guy's already offered a two-week hunt, next year, opening day, on the house, to make it up to you." He winked. "Next year you'll have your trophy."

He rose from the chair, smoothed his tie, and straightened his back. "So, we're clear," he said, his gaze intense, "you've had an exemplary career so far, outstanding even. Not one blemish. And I can count on you both to represent us on the task force?"

I nodded, my mouth hanging open again. There'd be no inquisition? No investigative hearing? All swept under the rug because the President had called?

"We'll see you back at headquarters then." He nodded to Dalton and headed for the door. "As soon as you are up and at 'em."

"Thank you, sir." Dalton's words followed him down the hall, then he turned his attention to me. "Are you happy?"

I nodded. "You're going to be all right."

"Yes, but I mean about the task force?"

I couldn't help myself. The thought of being on that elite team filled me with excited energy. I bounced a little on the bed, grinning like an idiot. "I can't believe it. Can you believe it?" I was going to need to let it sink in. "A presidential task force. Think of what we'll be able to accomplish."

"Government work." He rolled his eyes, teasing me. "It's all the same."

"I wonder what we'll be called. Maybe we'll have special berets. You'd look good in a beret," I said, teasing him back. "Maybe they'll call us The Green Berets—oh wait, that's taken. Maybe we'll have to come up with our own, secret name. Like—" I thought a moment "—Righteous Animal Crusaders against Evil."

"If the government gives it a name," he said, "it will be dull and practical, like, Task Force for Animal Enforcement."

"You mean like the SEALs? Sea, air, land."

Dalton looked at me with those eyes, those irresistible eyes. "Whatever it's called, if you're in, I'm in."

I shook my head, the emotions rushing back in. I hadn't been a good partner to him. "You were right. About the plane. That was a risky stunt I pulled."

He smiled wide. "I'm glad you did."

I relaxed a little. "Order a body bag. Was that supposed to be funny?"

The smile disappeared. "No."

"Don't ever say that again. Ever."

"Okay."

"I mean it."

"Okay."

"Because I—we—"

"I know."

I swallowed the lump in my throat. "I killed him, Dalton. I killed him."

He squeezed my hand. "I'm so sorry, Poppy."

"You were right about me. About..." I lifted my head, looked him in the eyes. "I'd do it again."

His eyes held mine.

"But now, with this—" My thoughts followed Stan Martin down the hall and the new assignment, the new team we'd be on. Together. Working as partners. "On the task force. We can't—"

"Kiss me."

I hesitated.

His eyes. "Kiss me."

I leaned down, my lips met his, and everything else floated away.

I nuzzled my face against his chest, felt the comforting rise and fall as he breathed.

"We'll figure it out," he said, stroking my hair.

But I knew better. We couldn't work together. Not as partners. We had let our guard down. We'd damn near gotten killed because of it.

I'd have to choose.

Thank YOU for reading. If you feel as strongly as I do about the issues presented in this book and you want to help, PLEASE start by taking a moment to post a review on Amazon.com and Goodreads.com and tell a friend about the story. Help me spread the word. For the animals!

If you'd like to learn more and stay in touch, please sign up for my newsletter or follow my blog at www. KimberliBindschatel.com

Author's Note

In 2012, on a wildlife tour boat in Resurrection Bay, I first learned of the infamous Butcher Baker, Robert Hansen. Our captain was pointing out landmarks and mentioned the maximum security prison there, telling us the story of an escape and, of course, of the well-known inmate and his sick obsession with hunting women.

I didn't give it another thought until I read the book, *The Blue Bear*, by Lynn Schooler. I highly recommend this beautiful story (if only I could write prose like that) about friendship and living in the Alaskan wilderness. Mr. Schooler endured his own tragic experience at the hands of Hansen and his telling brought the idea to life for me. I had been struggling with the theme of hunting, what fuels a desire to hunt, and Hansen's behavior seemed to fit.

I hope you enjoyed the story.

If you'd like to learn more and stay in touch, please sign up for my newsletter or follow my blog at www.KimberliBindschatel.com

THANK YOU

This dream of Poppy has come true with the help of many friends and family.

Thank you Carri for your guidance on criminal minds and helping me shape Rocky's character. Thanks to Loree and Jimmy Jensen of Trail Ridge Air of Anchorage, Alaska for checking my chapters on the bush plane flight. Any errors there are mine and most likely due to my dramatization. Thank you Monica Ashley for confirming my medical stuff.

Special thanks to Professor David Favre of the Animal Law Center at MSU for all the advice and guidance, and especially for the name of the new task force. As far as the law, any error is mine alone.

Poppy would not be Poppy, with that special pep, without Rachel. Thanks for always keeping me on track and for reading the same chapters over and over. And to Kathleen for the help with the outline. Alison, thanks for the German translation. Thank you to all my beta readers for the honest feedback: Alexa, Denise, Mom, Laura, Linda, Tricia, Erin, April, Barbara, Andrea, and Jan.

For, David, our little lumberjack, thanks for the long discussions on hunting and guns. Your enthusiasm for this story and our time together was a joy.

Thanks to my mom and dad for encouraging my love of animals from a very young age.

As always, a big, big hug and kiss to my loving husband, Ken. He knows how much this means to me.

ABOUT THE AUTHOR

Born and raised in Michigan, I spent summers at the lake, swimming, catching frogs, and chasing fireflies, winters building things out of cardboard and construction paper, writing stories, and dreaming of faraway places. Since I didn't make honors English in High School, I thought I couldn't write. So I started hanging out in the art room. The day I borrowed a camera, my love affair with photography began. Long before the birth of the pixel, I was exposing real silver halides to light and marveling at the magic of an image appearing on paper under a red light.

After college, I freelanced in commercial photography studios. During the long days of rigging strobes, one story haunted me. As happens in life though, before I could put it to words, I was possessed by another dream—to be a wildlife photographer. I trekked through the woods to find loons, grizzly bears, whales, and moose. Then, for six years, I put my heart and soul into publishing a nature magazine, *Whisper in the Woods*. But it was not meant to be my magnum opus. This time, my attention was drawn skyward. I'd always been fascinated by the aurora borealis, shimmering in the night sky, but now my focus went beyond, to the cosmos, to wonder about our place in the universe.

In the spring of 2010, I sat down at the computer, started typing words, and breathed life into a curious boy named Kiran in *The Path to the Sun*. Together, in our quest for truth, Kiran and I have explored the mind and spirit. Our journey has taken us to places of new perspective. Alas, the answers always seem just beyond our grasp, as elusive as a firefly on a warm autumn night.

Most recently, my focus has shifted to more pressing issues — imperiled wildlife. With the *Poppy McVie* series, I hope to bring some light into the shadowy underworld of black market wildlife trade, where millions of wild animals are captured or slaughtered annually to fund organized crime.

IT. MUST. STOP.

If you'd like to learn more and stay in touch, please <u>sign up for my newsletter</u> or <u>follow my blog</u> at <u>www.KimberliBindschatel. com</u>

The adventure doesn't end for
Poppy and Dalton

Join them in Mexico as they pursue turtle poachers in